WRENCH

AND OTHER STORIES

ALSO BY WAYNE HARRISON

The Spark and the Drive: A Novel

WRENCH
AND OTHER STORIES

WAYNE HARRISON

newamericanpress

Milwaukee, Wis.

newamericanpress

www.NewAmericanPress.com

Printed in the United States of America

ISBN 978-1-941561-09-6

Book design by David Bowen
Cover image courtesy of www.ifreepic.com

These stories have appeared in the following journals: "Least Resistance" in *The Atlantic* and *Best American Short Stories 2010*; "The Jump" in *The Sun*; "Wrench" in *New Letters*; "Wild Life" in *Other Voices*; "Storm Damage" and "Backlash" in *Crazyhorse*; "Rip Off" in *FiveChapters* (special mention in *Pushcart Prizes 2012*); "Between Gravities" in *Ploughshares*; "Divorced" in *Narrative Magazine*; "The Wreck" in *Columbia: A Journal of Literature and Art*; "Charity" in *McSweeney's* (notable in *Best American Short Stories 2009*).

For ordering information, please contact:
Ingram Book Group
One Ingram Blvd.
La Vergne, TN 37086
(800) 937-8000
orders@ingrambook.com

Praise for Wayne Harrison and *Wrench*

"Like Richard Russo, Philipp Meyer and Mark Slouka, Harrison understands the rusting body of American labor. Whether or not you love cars, Harrison speaks that special dialect so fluently that anyone with a heart can hear it."

— *THE WASHINGTON POST*

"Not since I read the stories of Breece D'J Pancake nearly thirty years ago have I felt so strongly about the debut of a writer of short fiction as I do Wayne Harrison. Among his many unforgettable characters are single mothers, young mechanics, ex-cons, recovering addicts and alcoholics, correctional officers, and a widower trying to do all he can for his toddler son. These stories crackle with a hard-earned and earthy specificity, one that suffuses Harrison's world with a light so authentic the reader cannot help but be transformed. But what I admire most about this superb collection is its profound humanity, its author's non-judgmental, compassionate, and unflinching gaze. Wayne Harrison is the real deal, and I will now read whatever he writes."

— ANDRE DUBUS III
author of *Dirty Love* and *House of Sand and Fog*

"Wayne Harrison has the rare ability to give us life as actually lived day to day, with all its threadbare passions, confusion, and shudders of almost-understanding. These are great stories, creating in a few thousand words whole worlds and lives. Harrison knows intimately the many ways we wear our lives thin then patch them up, again and again."

— JAMES SALLIS
author of *Drive*

"Wayne Harrison is an exciting new voice in American fiction."

— RON RASH
author of *Above the Waterfall* and *Serena*

"The world Wayne Harrison creates in his stories is filled with hard-working, big-hearted, folks who might've been fine if not for a wrench in the works of their life. With strong and straight sentences that remind me of Carver, and an authenticity to match the work of Breece D'J Pancake, *Wrench* is brutal and beautiful, tough and tender, and one of the finest collections I've read in years."

— ALAN HEATHCOCK
author of *Volt*

"Wayne Harrison is an extremely gifted writer."

— JILL McCORKLE
author of *Life after Life*

"Wayne Harrison's *Wrench* is one of the hardest-hitting collections I've read in years, a fierce, unsentimental evocation of working class lives. But reader, be advised: there's no tough-guy posturing here, no authenticity-as-affectation; instead, Harrison affords his characters their full human due, and finds grace in equal measure to disappointment and loss. An outstanding collection."

— ANTHONY VARALLO
author of *Think of Me and I'll Know*

"Devastating stories that hit like a hammer, again and again, with characters that walk off the page. *Wrench* has all the truth, drama, and emotional drive you could ever want out of fiction, without any of the pretense. Harrison is the best young writer I've come across in a long while."

— JONATHAN EVISON
author of *West of Here*

For Caye, Sabrina and Josie. Always.

TABLE OF CONTENTS

Least Resistance

NICK CAMPBELL WAS THE GREATEST HOTROD MECHANIC in Waterbury—some said in all New England. He owned a specialty shop that catered to high compression brutes from the muscle car era, Tri-power GTOs and Hemi Superbirds, rat-motor Corvettes and all the small block torque Detroit could dream up. Out of the Hole Automotive was sewn in midnight blue over the pockets of our work shirts, and pulling on my uniform each morning I felt transformed from pathetic teenager to minor superhero. Nick saw in me a capacity for technical imagination, which was enough for me to feel anointed, to covet his life and believe that I could one day receive it as my own.

So when Nick's jobs started coming back for warranty work in the summer of 1987, I was pretty devastated.

The first few rechecks were only mildly incriminating. A cracked spark plug that might or might not have been defective, a missing distributor screw that might or might not have been tightened. I convinced high-paying customers that their complaints were just normal breaking-in glitches, rather than shoddy work. But as word of Nick's unreliability began to spread, some of our formerly docile customers turned difficult.

One morning a '70 Monte Carlo, whose three-fifty engine Nick had beefed up with racing pistons, pulled right into the bays without a ticket. The owner was a stumpy, ruddy-faced Italian named Mimo. In a turtleneck and paperboy cap he tried to promote a rumor that one of his relatives was connected, though instead of a hard mobster Mimo looked more like Dom Deluise.

Nick, Tommy Costello, and I left our cars and approached the Monte from different angles. Tommy stopped to stretch with a fist in his spine, Nick lit a cigarette, and I tried to exude the same lack of urgency while Mimo got out and felt around in the grille for the hood latch. He stirred into the petroleum smell a sweet cologne that you couldn't get off all day if he shook your hand. "Something's leaking," he said. "I got oil drips all over my garage."

Instead of putting the Monte up on the lift, Tommy ("Tommy the Temper" as some of our regulars called him) kicked over a creeper and rolled under the front end with a drop light. At this point we could still hope that Nick's work wasn't to blame, that maybe it was condensation from the air conditioner and Mimo couldn't tell oil from water. We still had options. But when Tommy wheeled out from under the bumper, flat on his back and gaping at the chain-hung fluorescent light, he looked stricken.

"What?" Nick said.

Tommy sat forward and considered the blackened steel toes of his Wolverines. "Drain plug," he said, softly. Nick looked at him with such puzzlement that Tommy began to repeat himself.

"I heard what you said." Nick smoked his cigarette, his eyes glazing until, after a moment, even I hardly recognized him as the man *RoadRage Magazine* had deemed the "Maestro of V-8 Muscle."

"What's wrong with the drain plug," Mimo said. "He didn't cross thread it, did he?"

Quick as I'd ever seen him do anything, Tommy bucked off the creeper and headed for the toolbox that Mimo had the misfortune to be standing next to. When I saw the chrome flash of a wrench I thought for a panicked moment that Tommy might use it to crack open Mimo's head. Instead, Tommy asked if Mimo had any naked pictures of his wife.

His jowls flushed, Mimo glared at a slick of tranny fluid in the next bay. "No I don't. Jesus."

"You want to buy some?"

Mimo wadded his fat hands down in his pockets. "What is your problem, man?"

"My problem is a guy who pulls in here like he owns the place.

A guy always coming in for more cam, more carb, more this, more that, thinking it's gonna make his dick bigger, and then don't want to pay."

"What's wrong with the drain plug?" Nick said.

Tommy rubbed his oil-wet fingertips. "It's loose a little bit," he said, and he went back under the car with the wrench. Nick neglecting something so basic was inconceivable. Imagine leaving the house without putting on your right shoe.

Nick collapsed into a steel folding chair as his wife, Mary Ann, approached with a bookkeeping binder pressed to her slender waist. The eerie quiet from three mechanics in the same bay woke her from her trance, and she stopped short of the lobby door. "What's wrong?"

Nick didn't answer, and I watched her helplessly, a look of rejection, or maybe resignation, in her eyes that I felt in my own stomach. Just as she began to walk away, Nick said, "Do me a favor. Take Mimo out front and give him his money back."

"Whoa," Mimo said, a flattered, guilt-ridden knot of emotion now. "Hey, that's twelve hundred bucks. I'm happy with a discount."

"I don't give a damn what you're happy with," Nick said. He threw his cigarette in the trashcan, where any number of things could have gone up in flames.

What happened between Mary Ann and me started as conversations in the parts room. She'd ask me about my girlfriend, Katie, where I took her on dates, if I said nice things to her. When Katie dumped me a week before Christmas, I couldn't bring myself at first to tell Mary Ann. I was embarrassed and hurt, two things I didn't want to show, but when I finally broke Mary Ann and I had our first embrace between thermostats and Fram oil filters. It was a big hug that gave me a glimpse into where our friendship might lead.

Why I betrayed the one man in the world I wanted to become wasn't clear to me then—the summer I turned nineteen. Sometimes as Nick and I buttoned up a car he'd just brought back from the

dead, I'd promise myself it was over with Mary Ann. But then she'd
traipse out through the bays, not even noticing me as she started
an inventory, completely focused on her job, so strong to do that
when only days ago an orgasm I'd given her had made her cry. If
right then she told me to declare my love for her to Nick, I would
have. There wasn't much I wouldn't have done.

"Chant with me," she said late one morning on my day off. I
was naked still but didn't worry much about Nick coming home.
Even if the day arrived when Nick wanted to leave work early, he'd
never trust Tommy alone at the shop. Often Mary Ann and I didn't
put our clothes back on after making love—likely as not we'd fall
back into it after a while—and as she crossed the room to the stereo
I watched her back and ass and thighs. She had a body that didn't
disappoint me when she undressed, as had the two girlfriends I'd
been with, both of whom were thirteen years younger than Mary
Ann.

Mary Ann turned on stereo buttons as I contentedly looked
around their living room. In a silver-framed photograph over the
fireplace mantel, Nick stood arm in arm with Buddy "Leadfoot"
Baker. Shimmering baby-powder blue behind them was the 69
Daytona Charger that Buddy had broken 200 miles per hour with
at Talladega.

The other pictures were of Oregon, rolling waves framed by
Sahara-like dunes, a lake inside a dead volcano, white mountain
peaks, lava fields that looked like the face of the moon. Nick and
Mary Ann came out east four years before, when Nick inherited
the shop from a dying uncle. I imagined that arriving here, in
shitty Waterbury, from such a place as Oregon must've been like
waking from a dream.

Mary Ann plugged in a cassette, and the sound that rose from
the speakers was unlike any I'd ever heard. Two rich voices that
could only belong to gorgeous dark-eyed Indian women sang the
first chorus. *Om namah shivaya.* Then a hundred or a thousand

voices in unison. Behind the chant were the slightest sounds, tiny wind chimes, tiny buzzing. Then *om namah shivaya. OM NAMAH SHIVAYA.* You could hear tears in the women's voices, anguish, then resolve, safety. "What are they saying?"

"It's a salutation to that which we are capable of becoming." Mary Ann took my hand and brought me to the carpet, piled my legs in rough approximation of a lotus, and positioned herself beside me. I started to sway. It was warm, and we were naked together with this remarkable sound.

Then the phone rang. She let the machine answer, and the sound of Nick's voice in the house shot through me like a spark plug jolt. "Babe, I can't find the last Car Quest order..." When the message was over she turned off the chant tape, and we dressed in the silence of Adam and Eve after the apple.

Though she herself didn't drink, Mary Ann went to the kitchen and brought me one of Nick's Heinekens. It wasn't quite noon, but the day already had the feel of an epic journey for us, and all comforts were allowed. "Do you believe in karma?" I said. She watched me a moment, as to see where this was going, then nodded.

"What's a good way to improve it?"

"Go to college. Do something with your life."

I lit one of her menthols, a taste I'd already come to associate with these air-conditioned, self-indulgent mornings. "You sound like my dad."

With a small, brief smile she touched my wrist. "Sorry." She knew the story. My father told me, one morning before school six years ago, that he and my mother had outgrown each other—which was half true.

"And I like fixing cars."

"Maybe you'll find something you like better," she said. "Something kinder to your back and knuckles."

"Nick told me you used to work on cars."

She caught her lip in her teeth, and her mind seemed to change gears. "Do you like fortune cookies? I had one the other night that said, 'Spend much money on many doors.'"

I thought about that and shook my head. With a Chinese accent she said, "It mean go to *correge*. Open *possibiritries*." The next moment I spent in love with her, a feeling that both hurt and exhilarated me. She had a young, freckled complexion, and I was already losing hair in front, my teeth stained from cigarettes and coffee. I imagined the years between us were offset. I imagined— all I could do was imagine—that if anyone saw us holding hands on the street they would think we were the same age.

"Tommy Costello was human once," she said. "Don't take after him."

"Nick was actually who I was thinking of. All his rechecks."

She lit a cigarette for herself. "Justin, what do you think karma is?"

"Why bad things happen to good people," I said. And I thought, too late, of the baby boy they'd lost not even two years ago. But if I'd offended her she didn't show it as she brushed her permed, always-damp-looking red hair behind an ear and shaped the ash of her cigarette. "I don't think he can blame karma," she said. "Out of the Hole isn't a shop, it's a locker room. You guys aren't even nice to your customers."

This was often true—we modified engines for gearheads who tipped well and would've forgiven us for taking a shit on the floor if we juiced a dozen more ponies out of their hot rods. Tommy was the worst. Mary Ann had to buy a separate coffee maker for the bays just to keep him out of the lobby, where he got fingerprints everywhere and swore and farted as he pleased.

"It's the path of least resistance," she said. "There's no virtue, there's no discipline. And now his work is starting to suffer. I mean, where's the mystery?"

The first of two mistakes I made with Mary Ann happened during sex. I was starting to worry that she'd think missionary was the only position I knew, so I asked if we could try doggy style. She looked away and freed herself from me, turned over and waited, slumped over the sofa arm. The muscles in her back tightened, pulling down from her spine and causing her back to arc slightly. Entering her without the press of our fronts and without kissing was like breaking a spell. I apologized and turned her back, holding her fiercely and, as if I'd just pulled her from a hole in the ice, feeling her life return.

The second mistake was going into their bedroom. The door stayed closed when I was over, and one morning while she was in the bathroom I took a chance. The room was neat, the bed made—a rustic log bed of what I figured was Oregon fir. I stayed in the doorway. In a frame on the bureau was a picture of baby Joey, whose features were mostly Nick's with Mary Ann's electric blue eyes. Like a mini shrine the picture was surrounded by two plastic rings, a stuffed penguin, and a toy banana. In the mirror I saw something that drew me all the way in. Between the bed and window on the floor was a rumpled sleeping bag and pillow on a foam mat. The sight held me for some moments, and I was halfway back to the door when MaryAnn walked in.

"No, Justin," she said, and the pain in her voice sickened me. "I don't believe this."

"Mary Ann."

"Get out. " She came around and pushed me in the chest. "Just leave now. Go." She would have knocked me over had I tried to hold my ground.

This took us weeks to get over. In the hell of her silence I felt as low as Tommy, though unlike him, I was aware enough to experience the agony. I could see she was suffering as well, having no one to talk to other than customers and Nick, whose mind was generally passing from valve to cylinder to exhaust, like one of those tiny cameras that swim up veins on science shows. Then one day I got a sentence: "You had no right," and then, hours later, another, "I thought I could trust you." But slowly we came back together. One afternoon she drove out to Bethlehem, the little dairy farm town where I lived. We walked the downtown, three blocks of mostly antique stores, and in a coffee shop she explained Sudden Infant Death Syndrome, how it was every parent's nightmare, how she woke to the sight of Nick rocking the baby, pleading with him, "Warm up. Warm up, son."

Our small table had two chairs, and to slide around to her when her eyes glassed over would have been loud and clumsy. So I pressed her hand in both of mine and waited. In a while she managed a smile. "I didn't want to cry in here."

"Why does he sleep on the floor?"

"He dreams that Joey's still in bed with us, and then can't fall back asleep. He tells me not to take it personally, but my God. How do you not?"

Holding her hand in the coffee shop, I realized how close I'd come to blowing it with the one person in my life who needed me. Her family was back in Oregon. Her husband was distracted, about to lose his reputation and business if he couldn't get it together. And here I was, listening. Devoted to her and listening.

The rechecks were eating Nick alive. It wasn't the number of them—maybe seven or eight all summer—but that the mistakes were careless and often expensive. The only pattern was what you'd expect, that the jobs came in on our busiest days, when any of us were hard pressed just to keep our fingers out of spinning fans. For a while I fantasized that Tommy was behind it somehow, but on those chaotic days it was all I could do to keep track of myself, never mind watching him. And what did he stand to gain? We weren't known for competitive pricing and certainly not for customer service; all that kept us employed was Nick's fast-spreading reputation as a genius.

I gave Nick my full dedication, fueled by a dark secret to be the best friend I could. I intercepted pissed-off customers and lied straight-faced that a bad batch of spark plugs was to blame for their complaints. I put myself out on a limb, and it felt wonderful.

Early one afternoon Nick was helping me with a mid-seventies Formula that Firestone had sent by. They'd replaced the carburetor to the tune of five hundred dollars only to find that the idle continued to cough and skip.

Cylinders six and eight showed weak on a cylinder balance. Nick set one end of a long socket extension on the intake manifold and listened to the other end. He looked back to see the hydrocarbon count registering from the exhaust sniffer. It was up through the roof. "What do you think?"

"It needs a valve job," I said.

He brought the rpm up to 2000, held it, and the hydrocarbons dropped to passing levels. I was baffled. Worn valves are worn valves at any rpm.

Nick leaned back against my toolbox. He lit a cigarette off the head of one whose filter I could smell burning, he'd smoked it so far down. "You're how old?" he said.

"Nineteen on Friday."

"If you lived in Kenya, you'd be going on your first lion hunt."

"As long as I get a gun, not a spear," I said.

"They'd break eggs over your head in Germany."

"In America your boss takes you out for Jäger shots."

He grinned. "Figure this car out, and you got a deal."

I studied the KV screen again and ran another cylinder balance. I checked the ignition output and coolant level. Things that made no sense to check, I checked. I wanted to prove myself better than the mechanics at Sears.

"Nineteen," I heard Nick say to himself. He was facing the hopper window behind the oscilloscope, squinting as if in the sooty pane he could see himself at my age. But his nineteen was impressive, the age at which he balanced and blue-printed his first engine—scouring every surface, boiling, polishing, then torquing every fastener to spec. It was the most exhaustive engine work you can do, a feat I was light years from.

I advanced and retarded the timing until my eyes burned and I couldn't see the whirling slot mark on the harmonic balancer. I readjusted the idle speed. I looked at the work order one last time and finally lowered my head on my forearms over the fender mat. "Goddamn it," I said. "It's unfixable."

Nick picked up a ball-peen hammer, leaned on the passenger side fender, and tapped the EGR valve. Something held by suction dislodged, the engine coughed once and almost stalled, and he revved it clean. When he let go of the throttle, the engine idled like glass.

We waited to see that the fix held. The engine breathed quietly, and in the afterglow of witnessing a miracle I realized that the job wasn't going to make me any money. An EGR valve wasn't even a hundred-dollar ticket, so my commission—I made that plus seven an hour—would be less than five dollars.

Nick looked over the paperwork again. He stepped up to the Formula, and with one precise smack of the ball-peen he cracked the corner of the intake manifold all the way through. The engine began to sputter, and suddenly I was looking at a nine-hundred-dollar ticket. "It's on Firestone," he said. "Happy birthday."

Katie started calling the house. Six months after she dumped me she said it felt like losing her best friend. Finally I told her about my affair with Mary Ann just to scare her away. But Katie was persistent. "I'm worried about you, Justin," she said. "How old is she?"

"You meeting any guys up at UCONN?"

"It's illegal," she said. "If she's married, that makes it adultery."

"Jesus. What planet are you on?"

"I mean, how would you feel if you were him?"

"I already know how it feels, Katie." In December she'd left me for an ex-friend from Nonnewaug High. One night I saw his Le Mans parked in her driveway, blue icicle lights blinking over his hood.

I gave it a second to sting before I hung up. I thought that was it, but two days later she called and said she'd be there for me when this was over. I thanked her just to be civil, though I saw how impossible it was for us to be together again, how immature our love was. Life had always been easy and was going to continue to be easy for her. She didn't know the struggle of real people. But I was learning. In my heart I couldn't imagine it ever being over with Mary Ann.

I told her there was no chance in hell I'd ever go back to Katie.

"I don't blame you," she said. "You have to learn how to trust again."

I watched to see if she was relieved at all about my resolve. We held each other's eyes, and it was clear, when she leaned in and kissed me lightly, that she'd misread my sullenness. "Keep talking," she said. "Men never learn how to talk about pain."

I could see that it meant something to her to listen. "She was into jewelry," I said. "She had all these little jewelry boxes in her room, so I bought her this one giant one. It's like solid oak and four feet tall with swinging doors. But then she breaks up with me a week before Christmas. By the time I realize we're not getting back together, it's too late to return it. So I gave it to my mom, and now every time I walk by her room I have to look at that damn jewelry box."

As I spoke I watched the vertical blinds that closed us off from the daylit world, their color the soft red of fingers on a flashlight lens. I wondered if Mary Ann had seen how close I'd come to choking up. Yes, there was still some ache, but more than that I recognized that we were connecting yet again, more undeniable evidence that she and I were made for each other.

"Wait here," she said. When she came back from the bedroom

she handed me something smooth and cool. "It's a worry stone," she said. "To help you not be inside so much. Just let it take all the bad energy."

I rolled the stone, black-green like an avocado, in my palm. I recognized it but couldn't remember from where.

"Where did you feel it?" she said. "The hurt."

I looked into her big pale eyes. "It's like you forget how to breathe."

She took my other hand and pressed it to her bare chest. Her heartbeat was almost something I could hold. We stayed that way and her breathing deepened. She closed her eyes tightly, as if against a blast of sound, and a trickle of coldness seeped through me.

"Sometimes," she said, sitting forward. "God, it's like it just happened. Sometimes he'd nurse so hard it made me raw. I'd be in tears by the time he was done." She stared down at the old braided rug, with its frayed threads and little spills, and might have been looking into the past. "The morning after we lost him, I was so engorged I had to pump. My body didn't understand that he was gone. I pumped six ounces and then had to pour it down the drain. It killed me, Justin. I would've given anything for another bloody nipple."

I pictured her at the sink watching her milk seep away, my story a pathetic whimper next to hers. I looked at the stone again, and then it struck me. Looking for matches one day in Nick's box, the little top drawer where a mechanic keeps cigarettes, soda machine change, his Snap-on account book and receipts, I saw it, there way at the back, the twin of this little stone.

One night after hours Tommy, Nick and I were sharing a twelve-pack while Nick finished up on an '82 IROC Camaro. The engine was crawling with vacuum lines and sensor wires, and Nick's confidence had fallen to the point of sending me to Caldor for a Polaroid camera. He'd taken shots of the engine from several angles before dismantling.

"Your folks divorced?" Nick said, glancing at me over the

carburetor. I nodded, the question affirming how little he knew about me personally.

"How come your old man never taught you cars?"

"He's not like that," I said. "He buys new and sells when the warranty runs out."

"Man," Nick said, dolefully. "I don't know where I'd be without my old man taking me out to the garage. What kind of work's he do?"

"He's a, uh." I glanced at Tommy, who was leaning back on a metal stool with his legs open, a Milwaukee's Best on his thigh, just kind of staring off. "He's curator at a gallery in New Haven."

"Gallery?"

"Japanese art."

"What kind of art the Japs make?" Tommy said, perking up. "Rice cakes?"

"Robes. Swords, you know. Paintings."

"'Brown Stains on the Wall' by Who-Flung-Poo," he said and chugged his can. His mind was sharper than his vacant eyes and stubbled face suggested, and I grinned, though it was getting harder and harder to indulge him.

"I never got art," Nick said. "That Polack guy could throw cardboard under a dripping tranny and sell it for half a mil."

"Pollack," I said, and caught myself before I said his first name.

"He a bum chum, your old man?" Tommy said.

Nick laughed. "A what?"

"A sausage jockey. A backdoor commando." His look never varied from an expression of knowing that the world and everyone in it was full of shit. "Isn't that like how you qualify to be a curator?"

"He remarried," I said. "He has two kids." It shut him up but didn't erase that damn smirk. I stared at him. "I don't know, man," I said. All of a sudden my stomach was quaking, but the thought of how much Mary Ann despised him made me brave. "When was the last time you had a girlfriend, Tommy? You're not gay, are you?"

"I just had yours last night. Little Miss Pick-A-Hole."

"I'm serious," I said. "You need to get laid, man."

"Kid, you're going to mouth your way right into a hospital bed. I ever want your opinion, I'll get my little gimp niece to beat it out of you."

"All right, you guys." Nick said. "Play nice, now." He checked the timing and finished up the paperwork, and I didn't look at Tommy. "You want to," Nick said in a while, "go ahead and think of me as your stand-in old man. Surrogate, or whatever."

Tommy crumpled his can and tossed it in the box with the others. "Get a room, queers," he said. Watching him head toward the lockers, I felt I'd won. I got Nick a fresh beer. "Here you go, Dad."

He took it, grinning. "All right. Not Daddy, though. Or Pop. Call me Pop and I stomp a mudhole in your ass."

And after that night something changed in our relationship. Nick took on fewer cars so that he could give me jobs that were over my head and guide me through them. Not one of my cars came back, though a few of those he jumped on alone did. I saw that he cared more about my work than his own. I saw that karma, as Mary Ann had insisted, wasn't magical but just the natural course of things. He gave me what was abundant to him. He taught me how to listen to an engine as a compilation of sounds, the way dogs understand smell or wine makers experience taste. When his heart was open, and he was sharing all his secrets, I could only imagine the mechanic little Joey might have become.

Nick and Mary Ann decided the shop needed a face lift.

"Two-hundred bucks if you stay all night," Nick said to me, carrying four gallons of apple green latex from the trunk of his car. It was Saturday evening, half an hour after we'd closed. "Walls and floors," he said, "and it can sit and dry tomorrow. What do you say?"

What was to say? I ran down the alley to Lenny's Liquor Locker for a case of Heineken. Lenny Jr. served me without question, persuaded by my confidence even as I dropped my hill of fives and ones on the counter sign that said NO ID NO SALE. Back at the shop we spread tarps, pried off lids, filled the roller trays. Nick spun on an extension pole and then rolled so fast a green mist sprinkled his white Owner shirt. He overlapped where Mary Ann had edged and touched the ceiling a few times. Breathing hard, he dropped the roller on the tarp and lit a cigarette, pondering the rest of the wall, the thirty feet of it left to paint.

Mary Ann smoothed over his lap marks, and it was their quiet together that made me feel safe. You hoped for such assurance around your own parents. Mostly I remembered my father's light jabs, my mother's retaliations, words that hook in and stay.

"I thought you were good at everything, Nick," Mary Ann said, on tip toes stretching for the border tape.

Nick saw where he'd gone over half the wall thermostat. He grinned as when a random engine skip tried to outsmart him. "I get why Van Gogh cut his ear off."

"I like your ears," Mary Ann said. "Let's keep those. Maybe one of your big ugly hands."

And she didn't move even when his choking hands came around her throat.

"Now you did it," he said. "Now you're in trouble."

When I looked again at my own roller, fat green drips had run down to the floor. Sure there was a pang of jealousy, but also I could see that we were all changing for the better. These days, she was more animated around the shop and more affectionate with Nick, and when I laughed and cried I laughed and cried harder.

The phone rang in the lobby, and Nick said, "Benny about the Cutlass." The door hadn't even fully closed behind him when Mary Ann said, "I've got to tell you something incredible," and she took a bottle out of the case and held it out for me to open. I did, and she knocked my bottle in cheers before the first drink of alcohol I'd ever seen her take. She made a face. "I forgot how skunk cabbagey they are."

"They're strong," I said, for once feeling more experienced about something. "So what's incredible?"

"He got in bed with me last night. He slept right through to the alarm."

"Wow," I said, and I didn't see it coming, this shortness of breath. "That's really... I'm happy for you guys."

She had another sip and looked at me over the green bottle. "Justin," she said, "honey, we talked about this. Don't be jealous."

"I know. It's fine. We'll talk about it later," I said, ready to let the topic go as I dipped my roller.

"Talk about what?" she said. "What exactly do you mean?"

"Forget it," I said, her tone causing a dry lump to swell in my throat. "It's no big deal."

"No, you need to understand, Justin. I don't have to negotiate with you."

"That's not what I meant."

Nick came back out to the bays, but Mary Ann continued watching me, and for a panicked moment I thought she might continue our conversation. I set down my roller and cracked a beer for Nick. "All right, team," he said. "Let's make like Picasso."

Around midnight as the first coat dried, we washed up and drove to the Peking Duck in Nick's Chevelle. We feasted on beef chow mein and Mai Tais. Mary Ann was drunk and giddy, leaning on Nick's shoulder in the booth. When the fortune cookies came, and she tore up my "Financial news is in store" and wrote me one on a napkin, "Follow your heart. It will lead you home," I knew things were all right between us again.

After dinner we piled in the Chevelle, the three of us in front on the bench seat, and we raced into downtown Waterbury, with its restaurants closed and traffic lights blinking red. The cool night already smelled of fall. There was a half-mile straightaway from the south entrance of Bushnell Park to the north entrance, where Nick stopped the car. "We don't have seat belts on, remember," Mary Ann said.

"Do we ever?" Nick said.

I had no idea what the LS5 big block could do. Nick always babied it in and out of the lot, but now he dumped the clutch and mashed the throttle, and the car didn't move, the mechanical lifters tearing at the night like synchronized machine guns. Someone standing in front of the car could have pushed us back on the ice of melted rubber. The back seat filled with smoke as he shifted up the pattern. After a few seconds in fourth our momentum picked up gently, the tires finding purchase in the big gear, and we eased into sixty and then ninety. When the straightaway began to corner, Nick cut the wheel hard and pulled off a perfect 180 like you see in the movies. We thrashed around the interior, and I held on to Mary Ann. Nick reversed direction again. He finessed the counterslide with second gear and started another smoke show. At one point Mary Ann shouted over the engine, "I love this man!" We made four passes and left the historic downtown shimmering in Bridgestone black.

At the shop we finished off the case as we put on a second coat. It was my first time drinking myself sober, and I entered the light of day with a slow-lapping, enlightened mind. An ambulance siren grew loud, and we set down our rollers and through the bay door glass watched it race toward the interstate and lower valley towns. The sky had turned the swirling green of a shallow pond. Telephone poles and abandoned World War II factories floated into its wet light. Instead of rising, the sun rolled out of the furnaces of an old shell casings plant and filled its broken windows.

A week after the painting, the shop was bright and clean, the beer cans gone from the back ledge, little giraffes revealed—after a scrubdown with GoJo—on the bathroom wallpaper. Nick and Mary Ann came out to the bays together one afternoon. "Justin," Nick said, "you got a minute?"

Bent over a Grand Prix, I glanced from Nick to Mary Ann for signs that everything was, all of a sudden and horrifically, out in the open. "What's going on?"

"I wanted to tell you first while Tommy's on a test drive," Nick said. "He'll be pissed, but fuck him."

"What?"

"I just sold the place to Mitch Heedy at Firestone." He grinned at me and held up his hands. "Hang on, don't go having kittens. He's going to hire you on. We already discussed it."

"You sold it?" I said.

"We're moving back to Oregon. Mary Ann's brother wants me to manage a Performance Center of America out there. It's a glorified counter job, but it'll be less stress. Reliable income. Anyway, Mitch doesn't want Tommy, so try not to bust his ass about it."

The rest of the morning was a blur. Mary Ann stayed behind the counter helping customers, and finally I left her a note that was just a big question mark on a folded scrap.

She came out to the car I'd been trying to finish up for the past hour. "Where's Nick?" I said.

"In his office telling Tommy." She folded her arms and glanced away. Then she sighed and looked at me again. "Be happy for me. We deserve this."

"Why didn't you tell me?"

"You you you," she said. "That attitude won't make you very popular with women. You'll see." She smiled, but my expression made her look away.

"I'm not joking, Mary Ann. I mean, what the fuck?"

"Don't do this," she said.

"What's in Oregon?"

She blinked at me. "Our lives."

Suddenly the lobby door crashed into the adjacent wall and stayed there, the knob half-buried in the sheet-rock. Tommy marched out shaking his head, Nick not far on his heels. "Look, Tommy," Nick said.

"Motherfucker. Get away from me." Tommy kicked over a gallon of antifreeze and disappeared into the locker room. Then the metal crash that could only be the sound of a fist launching into a locker door. Again and again.

Nick closed the door to the locker room and turned to us. "Well, that didn't go as bad as I thought."

"Can I come out to Oregon?" I said.

When he looked at me his smile broke like a boy's. "Sure, you can come. You fish?"

"I mean, what's keeping me here?" I said. "What's the point without my Pop?"

"What'd I tell you about that?" he said and got me around the neck. We wrestled around before he pulled back, laughing. He wiped his eye. "All right. Keep it sad around here for Tommy's sake," he said and went back to the lobby, where he pulled the door knob out of the wall.

When he was gone my fingers went digging in my pocket for cigarettes, sticking one in my mouth, fumbling with a match. A couple of screwdrivers rolled off my fender mat onto the floor. Mary Ann was staring at me. "I don't think that's a good idea," she said, a surge of color in her face as she bent to pick up my screwdrivers. She brought them to my tool-box and started setting them in their holders. "I'm putting my marriage back together, Justin."

"He said I could come."

"This isn't your life." She went back to the car, beside which I'd wheeled a rolling tool tray, and started gathering up my wrenches and putting them away as well. And everything became clear to me. The cigarette fell out of my lips. "Jesus," I said. "It was you."

She stared at the floor where my cigarette had fallen. "Okay, Justin. What was me?"

"Sabotaging Nick's jobs. He wasn't fucking up."

Mary Ann sighed deeply and closed her eyes. She shook her

head, smiled bitterly, and then out of nowhere she lurched forward and slapped me. I'd never been slapped before, and it burned with the ring of a low piano chord. "You took advantage of a situation. That's it. That's all that happened." These things she said with a steady, calculated voice that made her anger all the more icy.

I didn't say a word. After she went back to the lobby I gathered sockets off the fender mat and tucked them in their plastic cases silently, as if in fear of waking someone. I didn't want to hear anything. The hammering in my chest was enough.

Divorced

DAN DRISCOL, MY FIRST SEX OFFENDER, LIVED WITH HIS MOTHER in a run-down colonial north of Watertown. I showed up unannounced for a knock-and-talk, and Driscol led me around little yap dogs through a network of tall, dismal rooms with shaded windows and argyle wallpaper. This was our preliminary meeting, the one that set the tone of my supervision, and I asked if we could take our business outside. I wanted to start off on the right foot. Driscol belonged with Special Management, but state cuts had slashed them down to skeleton crews, and my office was pulling some of the load.

He brought me out on the front porch to a wooden picnic table, where we sat in shafts of light splaying through a chokecherry tree. Driscol was smaller than most of my guys, doughy but thin shouldered with pencil arms poking out of his short sleeves. You wondered how he'd gotten by for thirty months at Osborn. Under a CarQuest cap his pale eyes pulled into his cheeks like buttons in a vinyl chair. He talked about his job, which was delivering auto parts to repair shops in town, and the radio talk shows he drove around listening to. "Rush. Hannity. Savage Nation, and them Air America ones for the other side. It gets to where I sort of crave it on the weekends."

From my time in corrections I remembered sex offenders ("snappers" or "weenie-wavers" to the overworked C.O.) as a gloomy bunch, moping like zombies around their segregated day rooms. But Driscol was eager and talkative, making my job easy when I needed it easy. Yesterday in the mail I'd received the final papers of my divorce. It was official, no eleventh hour reconciling, but still I wore my wedding ring in to work. Most of my cons were single men, some divorced themselves, a few with a restraining order between them and the women they still loved. When I wore the ring it said that I was fortunate in this part of my life, at least, and sometimes I'd catch them staring at it, their eyes full of yearning.

Driscol asked if he could smoke. I nodded and he lit a Parliament with a wave of lighter, fast as a magic trick. Not long into the interview, he made the mistake of asking about my time in the military. "I appreciate how you didn't need the draft," he said. "That's how a patriot does it. Volunteers. I just about signed up in ninety. I even told my boss I was going to Desert Storm."

I waited for him to finish. I don't speak loudly with my guys, I don't compete or interrupt, though I speak intently. "Who told you that about me?"

He sat straighter on the bench. "Neil Hammond. My first PO."

"Officer Hammond knows better," I said. "We need to be clear that these meetings are only about you."

A maroon stain began to spread up his throat. He nodded and looked at his hands on the picnic table top. "I'm sorry, Ed."

"And for the time being, I need you to call me Officer Green."

"Okay, God. I'm sorry, Mr. Greene—Officer Greene."

"It's okay, Dan. We're just laying out some ground rules." I opened my folder, and he smoked quietly while I skimmed a few notes. My first question was about his victim, a junior at the high school where he had worked as a janitor. "She was one of the ones I used to get alcohol for," he said. "I had me this break room in back of the furnace, and she'd come around at lunch sometimes. I'd let her have smokes, too. Man, was I asking for it. I guess just to feel popular was why it happened." He made steady eye contact as he spoke, pausing only to glance at the tabletop, where his thumb rubbed a shallow depression in the wood. "We'd be back there talking. Normal stuff about like her classes and her folks and everything. I don't know when, but somehow it got me turned around. All of a sudden I thought I was in love. That's how I mean turned around. I thought later on, when she was out of school and eighteen and everything. Maybe we could start off just being friends and see. But pretty soon she got this boyfriend and didn't come around no more. That sort of… man, I don't know. I saw a whole nother side of myself I didn't know was there."

The felony he went on to describe matched the one I'd read in his case file. (A surprising number of them try to sell you less offensive versions.) I noted that he didn't try to say, for instance, that she came on to him or was otherwise asking for it. He slipped her Rohypnol at a logging trails party, then carried her into the woods and raped her while her boyfriend was on a beer run.

I was satisfied with his attitude of acceptance and accountability, and I started drifting in and out of the interview, which was unlike me. I'm nothing if not focused. But I found myself thinking about Rose Darcy, who had resurfaced in my life a few weeks ago. We'd dated in high school, and I'd found her on one of those online reunion sites. I remembered the kids we'd been at a small Vo Ag school, surrounded in the fall by corn-stalks where teenagers could smoke or make love while an exhausted Ag teacher (they were moonlighting farmers) demonstrated how to back up a two-wheel wagon. Rose and I at the creek, or sharing grain alcohol cherries in the hay mow—dropping a few down to the old blind palomino.

Driscol sat quietly, scraping his shoe into the blistered deck paint. I looked at the ant tracks my pen had drawn up the page. "How do you feel about what you did?" I said.

He looked up at me and sighed. He pulled off his cap and was bald except for a rim of dull brown hair that wrapped around his head like packing tape. Setting the cap on the table he scratched his freckled scalp. "They had me on suicide watch almost a year. That was, I don't know, like you want to just wake up out of a bad dream all the time. I'm not like that no more—they had this really good lady psychologist at Osborn. But what I feel about it now? I mean, I hope she can forget. Not forgive or anything, but just forget me. That she can have a normal life and get married. Be in love and be happy."

The front door opened behind me, and Driscol pulled his cap back on. His mother set half a liter bottle of Virgil's Root Beer and two glasses of ice between us. She was in her seventies, with the big muscular hands of a farm wife. She nodded when I thanked her. With her own pack of Parliaments, she hobbled over to a corner of the porch not far from us and smoked.

Driscol poured carefully, tipping the glass so it didn't foam over. It was a good heady root beer, and we wiped off mustaches with the backs of our hands.

"What's happening socially?" I asked. "Are you dating anyone?"

He held up his finger and looked over at his mother. "Okay?" he said.

She leaned against the corner post with her arms folded, letting us know she wasn't going anywhere. It seemed to be her place to smoke.

"Ma, you know this is my private meeting."

"What're you going to say that I don't already know, Mr. Bigshot? You think you got secrets?" Then she turned to me and said, "I could give you some conditions." I watched her as patiently as I could manage, and with an exhale of smoke she said, "On his parole. Like mowing that hay field in the back yard. Getting firewood now so we don't have to throw it on green." She had two long drags and snubbed out the cigarette, apparently satisfied with her little production, and went inside—for good, I hoped.

Driscol shook his head in submission as he knocked off his ash. "She just mopes around most of the time anymore," he said. "With Dad gone, and Aunt Katy on hospice now. But what you asked about, no. I don't meet nobody, Officer Greene. Not in my job."

"Remember that if you do start a relationship, you'll need to tell them about your history," I said. "At least, while you're on parole you will."

His mouth loosened, and he nodded. "The whole point is being yourself around somebody."

There were moments when you saw them going inside themselves, forgetting you were there. He tapped out his cigarette and sighed again, blinking at his coupled hands. I made a note to tell him something about my time in Kuwait. Once a Norwegian intelligence officer was arm-wrestling a guy in my fire team over the hood of our Humvee. They'd been in a dead heat about five minutes when a shot rang out from the hills, and the Norwegian lost half his thumb to a 7.62 mm round from a sniper rifle. Craziest thing I'd ever seen over there. I'd save that story as a reward for Driscol if he kept behaving.

I finished a last note and opened my briefcase. My Beretta waited in its leather scabbard, and I slid his case file on top of it. "I'm searching your bedroom today, so I hope it's clean."

He started to get up, but I motioned him to stay. "Upstairs, second door on the right," he said. "And while you do that, I ought to...?"

"Drink your root beer. I'll need you to fill a UA cup before I go."

He grinned with embarrassment and looked out at the street. "You bet," he said.

If Driscol smoked in his bedroom, the old plaster walls didn't show it. The bed was made, a pair of sandal slippers pushed up to the box spring. The walls were empty except for a muscle car calendar from the parts shop where he worked. In a way it reminded me of my own bedroom at Patriot Arms in Bristol, where I'd been living since the fall. No TV, no stereo—a place where you went to check email and sleep and nothing else.

I turned on the computer and looked at what he had between brick book-ends, mostly science fiction and fantasy, two hardcovers on key marine battles in Vietnam. I picked up a few by their spines and shook them over the carpet. From one, a postcard from Key Largo, postmarked twenty years ago: *Hey Dan. Having a blast. Miss talking to you. Stacey*

I checked his internet history. News sites, a study site for Automotive Service Excellence certifications, a chat room for evangelical singles—I wished he would've mentioned that, but it was minor. Then I got on Yahoo and checked my email. Nothing new, but I pulled up an email Rose had sent a week before—just a short thank you for our first date. She couldn't wait to see me again.

As I was getting out of the chair I caught a whiff of peppermint. Instinctively, from my years as a corrections officer, I scanned the plaster wall until I found it. Cons in prison would chip out cavities in the concrete walls to hide roaches, shanks, whatever they could fit, and cover it back with toothpaste. Driscol had done a careful job. I dug into the crater with a pencil and found an Attaché memory stick.

The pictures were taken in the woods. One girl was urinating by a tree, smiling at the camera. One was standing in a clearing naked from the waist down, holding a Bartles & Jaymes wine cooler. The oldest girl might have been fourteen.

Driscol was slumped forward on the passenger side. I drive an old F150 pickup with just lap belts, and he could pull away from the seat back when the handcuffs started cutting in. I'd warned him not to talk on the ride, but when we were still a few miles outside Waterbury, he said, "What kind of dog do you have?"

"Shut your mouth," I said, stupid and tongue-tied. I'd completely misread him. In eight months he would have been a free man. Now every little sound he made was a gunshot at close range. He looked back out the window, which was covered with nose prints from Whitaker, the black lab Brenda got along with the house. Every other weekend was my weekend, as if Whitaker were a child in a custody arrangement. I hated Driscol's knowing even that there was a dog.

It took about an hour to process him, and from the East Main parking lot of the Waterbury station house, I found myself dialing my old phone number. Brenda answered on the second ring. It was quarter after five, and she must've just walked in the door. Her purse—the Louis Vuitton I'd bought her on our fifth anniversary—would be on the breakfast bar with her keys. She'd be standing in front of the garden window, looking through the basil and cilantro to the budding roses in the back yard.

"What's wrong?" she said, having heard it in my voice. "Ed?"

"Are you free tonight?"

"Am I …?" she said, but caught herself. "No. Tonight isn't good. What happened? Did something happen?"

But by then I could barely find my voice. Tonight wasn't good. She was only human, and lonely like me, but I felt bitter and ended the call in a way that would leave her wondering, maybe even doubting herself. Then I called Rose, who was happy to hear from me. She was still at work but liked the idea of my coming over. "You can meet Zoe," she said.

I bought a pack of Camels, smoked three all the way down, then stopped at my apartment to wash off the smell. Dusk filled the unlit rooms. I showered and got out fast.

Rose lived on a street lined on both sides with turn-of-the-century triple-deckers, not unlike those I'd been in hundreds of times on my knock-and-talks: you took the far left door on the porch (she'd left it unlocked; I locked it behind me) and then up two flights of barking, cracking wooden steps between knotty paneling—an overpowering smell of wood. The stairs ended on a landing with a window, coat hooks, a washer and dryer, the baby smell of fabric softener. And there you stood in a strange limbo, both inside and outside the apartment.

Under the door was half an inch of space, and I could hear voices. Little Zoe hollering, "I *know* where it is!" The TV. Sink water running. Sounds that were the opposite of loneliness.

Rose opened the door with a hand towel on her shoulder. "You found us," she said. Zoe was there at her knees. "Mommy got snowed on at work," she said, and she started to roll her butterfly print T-shirt up her belly.

"Don't do that," Rose said. "Eddie won't stay if you don't behave."

Zoe slid from foot to foot. She had strawberry bangs and a little freckled nose, dark eyes like her mother, as cute as you could imagine.

"One of the glue guns at work exploded on me," Rose said, turning in the light. The left side of her hair was speckled white—it really did look like snow.

While Rose showered, Zoe took my hand and escorted me into the parlor, a round room with a panning view of Franklin Street. Over flaring brake lights the windows were even with courthouse flags billowing to the west, and a heavy, bruise-colored sun stained the haze at the back of the sky. "I like your view," I said.

Zoe let go of me and climbed over the arm of a corduroy chair that was in the fully reclined position. As if she were alone in the room she stared at an episode of *King of the Hill* on TV. I wasn't in the mood for sitting and looked over the artwork that had come, I assumed, from the frame shop Rose managed. I recognized a Monet and two Picassos. The Degas and the Matisse I had to go over to and read.

As I took a seat on the futon, Zoe said, "Do you like butterflies better, or elfs?" She leaned over the recliner arm to look back at me.

"Butterflies or elves?" I said, trying to read which way she was leaning.

"Little ugly elfs, or butterflies."

"Oh, butterflies. That's an easy one. Every time I go outside, the first thing I do is look around for butterflies."

She ran her hand down to a little tear on the side of the recliner, then suddenly looked back at me. "But what *kind* is your favorite?"

"Well, they're all pretty. But I guess I'd have to say monarchs are my favorite."

"I like blue ones." She rolled back around in the chair.

There were open coloring books on the floor. A plastic star that went to something. A stuffed dolphin. On one of the window sills a small calico was trying to sleep, but every minute or so it opened its eyes and looked in Zoe's direction. I settled back watching TV and felt almost drowsy.

One of the *King of the Hill* characters belched, and Zoe started laughing. I liked the show, but watching it with a five-year-old, I found myself squirming on the futon. "Hey, Zoe—"

"My real name's Amanda," she said, "and Mandy's my nick-knack name. I'm only Zoe *now* so I can see if I like it better."

"Okay, well. I like them both," I said. "Which should I call you?"

"I don't *know* yet. I'm still making my decision." A timer went off in the kitchen and Zoe reached down for the handle that closed the footrest, but she couldn't get it to move, and she climbed out of the chair open, the way she'd climbed in. She ran out of the room, and then her footfalls stopped suddenly.

"You hafta come see if the chicken's pink," she called out. "Don't you want to race?"

After Zoe was in bed, Rose and I shared a bottle of Zinfandel on the futon. Zoe, she told me, was actually Zoe's middle name. Her father had picked Amanda—the name of one of his old flames, Rose had found out too late. After six years he divorced Rose and married this old Amanda.

"I actually got an invitation to the wedding," she said. "Just his little way of demonstrating how totally pathetic he is." She pressed her painted thumbnail up under one of her front teeth, a habit derived from biting her nails when we were in high school. She'd changed into a sheer, pretty blouse and light colored jeans. "And anyway," she said, "Zoe *is* a prettier name."

"It is," I said.

The calico jumped up in her lap. "This is Freebie, who Zoe loves to terrorize." She dug in as only a cat's owner can, raking hot spots until the animal was revving with its mouth open. "You don't have pets?" she said.

"A black lab every other weekend."

"That's right. You told me that. Maybe you should get something, just for you."

"I figured if I could get through a divorce without a pet, I could survive anything."

"That sounds a lot like torture. And you do it on purpose?"

I had to laugh. I thought how twenty years ago, Rose and I would have jumped at the chance to move out of our parents' homes and live alone. She was more hesitant now, which was only natural. Single motherhood. Who wouldn't be more hesitant?

"At least get a fish," she said. "That's a tiny bit of company, but you still can't cuddle with it. So that could be your deprivation, or whatever."

As suddenly as the cat came to her, it sat up, jumped off and disappeared down the hall. Rose wiped off her lap and we sipped our wine. A muted crime drama played on the TV across from us.

"Does it bother you to tell people you're divorced?" I said.

She rocked her glass a little and laughed. "What I hate is admitting I married him in the first place."

"Everybody in my family's divorced and single except one uncle, who's on his third wife."

"Nobody can say what happiness is. Isn't that the moral of the story?"

"You know how many cons I meet with every week?" I said. "Thirty-seven."

"Is that a lot?"

"It's all I can handle. And you know how many of them are happily married? One. One old guy who wrote a few bad checks, who shouldn't have gone to jail in the first place. That's it. The rest are alone or stuck in these awful codependent relationships."

"Maybe you should just get another job," she said. "I mean, if it depresses you."

"I used to feel like I was good for them. Proof that marriage could actually work." I looked at her and realized what she'd said. "I don't know what else I'd do."

"I could probably give you some advice. I'm the queen of career changes." She finished her wine and set the glass down. Then she looked at me and said, "Do you and your ex still talk?"

I nodded.

"Do you?"

"Sometimes."

"And is she pretty? I bet she is."

The question threw me. She smiled, and I felt a welling in my chest. She leaned back and looked up at the ceiling, as if she had no secrets anymore, and for a few moments she closed her eyes. I reached for her hand and said, "You've got nothing to worry about." I meant it, but it came off hokey.

She sat forward with a little grin, something less than a smile. "No, being divorced doesn't bother me," she said. "I'd have to say my big disappointment in life is not going to college. Not having that experience. At the shop they hire kids from Post and UConn all the time. Just sales kids or stockers. And they have this attitude like they want you to know it's just beer money. They have no freaking clue what real life is like."

"They'll find out soon enough," I said.

"When I moved I thought it would be way out west," she said. "Someplace dry with white mountains in the background. I made it to Danbury for three years. That was my big move." She blinked at some crayon marks on the coffee table.

"I think you even went a little east," I said.

"You asshole," she said, and clobbered me with a stuffed giraffe.

The other furniture in her bedroom was a nicked-up dresser with an oval mirror, a black vinyl chair, and a book case by the window. But the bed was all you saw, a great island of mattress that came up waist high, to the very top slats of the blonde headboard. It had carved-pineapple head and foot posts with a canopy, and sheer side curtains drawn back. I took off my shoes and climbed up on it. From a ledge of chocolate-trimmed pillows I looked up at the lilac canopy, feeling like I was in a cartoon.

"The mattress is organic latex," Rose said. "Whatever that means." Across the room, she began taking draped slacks off the handle bars of an exercise bike. "Like my three-hundred dollar clothes hanger?"

"No cleaning allowed," I said. "Get over here."

She hung the slacks in the closet and turned. Her arms swayed in the air and she lowered them. She didn't seem to know what to do. It wasn't going to happen as easily as when we were kids, that was clear now. We'd just bought into the fiction that it would.

"Hey," I said, to move us past the moment.

"Hey, yourself." She started opening the bottom snaps of her blouse. "Do you realize this is the first time we're doing this legally? I could have had you arrested."

"And I could have had you arrested."

"Why don't you take your clothes off, Mr. Parole-man?"

I sat forward and ripped the shirt out of my pants.

"I'm breaking my own five-date rule, just so you know."

"As in, no nookie for five dates?"

"But I think we deserve this."

"We earned it," I said.

She stopped unsnapping. "Earned it how?"

We watched each other, both of us waiting to see what the moment turned into. I smiled. "I don't know why I said that."

"I think you're just giddy." She turned around and worked off the jeans with her back to me. This was how we would undress, at a distance, and maybe that was easiest—without the kissing and cross-fumbling of arms. We didn't need to show the size of our desire. We'd already proven that in high school. Her thighs were heavier, her ass a little flatter, but so what? A glance at her backside and I was ready—thawed from the deep freeze. She slid the blouse off her shoulders and wriggled back a hand for the only thing left, the clasp. Then it was just the pink memory of the bra straps on milky skin.

I lay back and slipped out of my pants. The jar candles smelled like vanilla and coffee and made a little movie on the wall. When I sat up again, she turned and came toward me in a slow ascending way, as though she were emerging from a pool. Her breasts were round and high. The bra hadn't been doing anything at all. She saw how I was staring and looked down. "So, yeah, these are after-market," she said. "Gary paid for them. After Zoe was born, they got, you know. He was such a—" She shook her head and looked at me. "Am I ruining this?"

"They're nice, Rose. You look nice."

"This should be the easy part." She came to the bed and helped me with my undershirt. "Look at you. You still work out." She ran her warm fingers over my chest. "You win the 'Most Likely to Look Exactly the Same' contest."

Rose turned her head down and I combed my fingers through her hair. After my boxers were off she knelt in front of me. I wasn't expecting this, could recall it only once when we were dating. She was aggressive, and when she looked up and asked if I wanted her, I couldn't help but think that someone had taught her to do it this way. The idea made me restless. I said yes, and it all felt wrong.

Then the door pushed open and Zoe walked in.

"Jesus." I grabbed at pillows to cover myself.

"Easy," Rose said. "Take it easy."

Zoe had dragged in a little fleece bathrobe. "It's cold, and we have to go inside now," she said, still in a dream. "It started to snow."

"Honey, it's not snowing," Rose said and seemed to endorse the idea of doing nothing about this. Her voice was soft, unalarmed.

I felt sick. I rolled off the bed all that distance to the hardwood, cracked my knees, and swore before I could stop myself. Zoe let out a wail.

"Ed, Jesus," Rose said.

I peeked over the high mattress. Zoe saw me and wiped her eye.

"Talk to her," Rose said. "She's not going to remember any of this."

But I couldn't speak. Little Zoe squinted at me in the weak nightstand light. And I thought that what she was seeing would be the end of her childhood. Her mother naked with a man Zoe had known for only a few hours this night.

"Okay, don't say anything," Rose said. She took Zoe's hand and walked her toward the door. Just before they were out Zoe turned mid-step and glared at me like an avenging angel with the wrath of God in her eyes.

I put on my clothes and sat in the swiveling vinyl chair—it must've been out of an office. I looked at the room and saw myself in it as if from overhead, hunched forward, my legs spread. It was a place I would never have imagined myself in even a year ago. Trying to make something work with a single mother, pretending I knew anything about kids. The judge at our divorce proceedings, when we told him we had no children, had said, "I'm glad to hear that," and I remember taking a small sense of pride in our failure being limited to us alone. For a few moments, until I was able to force the thought from my mind, I wondered where Driscol's mother had gone wrong with him.

Rose came back dressed in a terry-cloth robe she must've had in the bathroom. She stopped a few feet into the room, looked at me, and then walked to the window. She watched outside and didn't turn around. Above us a quarter-mile away, headlights drifted over the Yankee Bridge out of town. "You're dressed," she said. "You must be leaving."

"I guess I am." It was a trashy situation straight out of the life of one of my cons. I went over to the bed and picked up my shoes, dropped one, picked it up again, my head spinning from the wine each time I bent over.

"You know, you have this thing now," Rose said. "This—I don't know—you act like you're better than I am."

"How about we avoid a fight," I said. "Let me just go home."

"I can see it in the little ways you say things. You seem like any minute you're going start with the put-downs. I don't remember that about you."

"I'm not the only one who's different," I said, and she came up behind me and closed the door. "Keep your voice down," she said. "You didn't see the look on your face just now. Like you were... I don't know. Disgusted."

"How hard is it to lock a door?"

"Sometimes kids see things they shouldn't. It happens. At least it does in my world."

I sat in the vinyl chair and put on my shoes. Between us a dull band of street light lay across the braided rug. Rose finally turned and walked past me, to the dresser where she opened the top drawer. She took out a purple velvet bag—a Crown Royal bag—and dug around inside it. Now and then a cold glance at me as she proceeded to load a glass pipe. "The truth is, I don't think I have another shitty controlling relationship left in me," she said. "I don't know what this is. I know I liked us better then. I wish it could *be* then."

She went back to the window, lifted it open and then sat on the wide sill.

Twice I started to get up to leave, but then I didn't know if there would be any coming back, or if I wanted there to be. I sank in the chair. She lit the pipe and blew the smoke out through the screen. She was quiet for some time before I saw her hand raise up to her face, wiping away tears. "Goddamn this," she said, and that was all.

When she finished smoking she took the pipe into the

bathroom, flushed the toilet, and then put it back in the dresser. She took off her robe and pulled on panties and a T-shirt. Then she just got in bed, turned out the light, facing the window, her back to me.

Quiet was all I could manage, and I felt no urge to move. Just sitting there watching her breathe, I pictured my guys in rooms like these—no clear faces, but the slump, the feet, the slant of dingy light lipping in from outside. I waited for an impulse, a desire, anything. A long while I waited, but nothing would come.

The Jump

CHARLIE CAME TO THE DINNER TABLE WEARING EYEGLASSES without lenses. The frames were the same pillow shape as his mother's, though hers were apricot and these a red tortoise shell like a movie star might wear. Where did he get them? The obvious answer was Mrs. Dugan. During the summer she watches him while I'm at work, and they look like the kind of glasses—eccentric, free spirited—she might wear.

They kept walking down his nose as he leaned in for bites of sloppy joe. "I'm thinking those might be a little big on you, bud," I said. He shook his head, and the glasses tumbled into his lap.

"Zipper needs a bigger place to swim," he said and slipped them back on by their end pieces, as if he'd been wearing glasses all his life.

"Tetras like small tanks," I said.

"I think he wants a pond."

"You mean you want to let him go?"

"No, like dig a pond. Then we could go outside to visit." This time as he looked up at me through the lopsided frames, I saw the articulate, reasoning young man he might become.

"He'd freeze in the winter," I said.

"Not if you heat it like pools are."

"Are you ready for the diving board on Sunday?" I said, changing subjects myself for one I knew would trump any more talk of Zipper and ponds.

Charlie sat up in his chair, his eyes shifting, at the same time brave and afraid, and then something else, a grown-up emotion, or did I imagine this? His face turned solemn with the weight of delivering on his first big promise. "I'm gonna do the new record," he said.

*

Three days later we're crossing the dewy lawn of the Woodbury town pool, Charlie in his trunks with a Sponge Bob towel stuffed cape-fashion into his T-shirt, on a comfortable July first morning.

Racked over the lifesavers, an emergency hook extension pole catches Charlie's eye. Pushing up the glasses, he stares himself right into an azalea hedge. He checks to see if I'm giggling, stomps bark mulch off his sandal, and then his eyes sail across the deep end to the diving board. His mouth opens.

To date Charlie has jumped into four feet from an Oxford dictionary, and five feet from a block of plywood on which "Town of Woodbury" is painted. Every weekend a little deeper, a little higher. Sometimes in the wake of his jumps, a halo of bubbles where the water takes him, swimmers in the shallow end will sing out and bob in their water wings.

But it's not the esteem of shallow-enders that drives him to the diving board. This day, Sunday, would have been Sharon's birthday, her big thirty-five. The jump into the deep end is Charlie's present to her.

We pass through the chain-link gate and he walks it quarter-circle back, a decisive bell tone as he sets the latch. Our sandals clap together on the combed cement, Charlie's nervous ribbon of footwork, my own bee-line between him and the pool ledge. It's nine-thirty, and under the blue morning sky webs of fog lift off the heated water.

Holding the chrome rail at the shallow end, Charlie taps the water with his toe until circles enlarge like cartoon radar, and dips his foot in. A sign behind him reads NO GLASS NO RUNNING NO HORSEPLAY.

I wave to Mark in the lifeguard chair. The sun still faint as a light bulb, Mark wears a windbreaker he'll shed when the first high school girls arrive. A blue nylon rope halves the pool, its Styrofoam footballs riding wavelets of a lone swimmer. A man of seventy or more, he laps sidelong, touching the five foot marks as if they were stop clocks in a chess game. The crown of white hair hugs his skull, follows its nodes and depressions. He stops only to pull sheets of water down his face, his long-fingered hand the color of a paper bag. He notices neither my son nor me.

Charlie pushes the glasses up into his hair, and I find myself relieved that the other kids haven't come yet. After this jump, after Charlie has overcome his last challenge at the pool, we'll talk about getting rid of the glasses. Maybe I'll bargain with him, buy him proper-fitting sunglasses, less extravagant ones that might spare him some teasing.

Charlie finds three lounge chairs huddled away from the others at the far end of the pool. On the center chair, he sits and crosses a leg to remove his sandal heel-first the way he's seen me take off cap-toe oxfords a hundred times. He peeks behind his waistband where the shoelace bow still holds, and then, out of busywork, he looks to me. He stands once, twice, sits again.

"There's plenty of time," I say. I open my towel to receive car keys, wallet, T-shirt, and make a roll of it all. He joins me on my chair and we lie back under a small, story book sky. I wonder how long it will be before he outgrows the cradle between my arm and chest. A morning breeze picks up, lifts his hair against my chin, and we're back at Walgreen's a month ago. Charlie came over from the shampoo aisle holding a denim blue bottle of Finesse. "This kind," he said and dropped it in the cart.

"That's not what you want." I fished the bottle out. "For permed hair, see? Grab some Pert. You like Pert."

"*This*," he said, loud enough to draw the stares of two women in cosmetics.

I could have yelled at him then, though I'd promised myself never again, a reasonable promise, and in an even voice I asked if he wanted his hair to be curly. It was close enough to a lie that my face warmed with shame.

Charlie took the bottle from me and dropped it back into the cart.

Now as I run my fingers through his fine sandy hair I smell them both. A coating in back of my throat begins to melt. "We're pretty tired," Charlie says, sinking back. He says this lately when he lies beside me. He searches the morning sky, where high cirrus clouds pass through one another like misguided angels.

Sharon and I explored religions with Charlie. The three of us attended a weekend retreat in upstate New York, where we chanted before a Buddha statue the size of a phone booth. Sikh friends shared their faith over onion chutney. We thought we'd open all doors for him, but when he finally needed answers all I could offer was by-the-numbers Christianity. Charlie imagines all the angels reclining on cartoon clouds, watching over us.

Mark the lifeguard is a family friend, paperboy, autumn leaf-raker. He turned stoner in his senior year of high school, and I don't know if I trust him to save Charlie if it came to it, but I'm here, and Mark means well. High in his white ladder chair he's paging through *Motor Trend,* generously unaware of Charlie's worried approach to the board, though he'll be the first one clapping after the jump. I remember Mark at my door that afternoon, without his ubiquitous Red Sox cap, one hand clamped on the other's wrist in a show of condolence as generic as his opening sentence: "If there's anything I can do, Mr. Pierce." But he's not too young to mean what he says, so I hold him to it. I ask favors. His eyes glisten with Visine. In Sharon's closet he picks out clothes for his older sister, who is in the Czech Republic on a Fulbright.

In the winter I sent him to Star Auto Wrecking with the signed title to Sharon's Celica. He brought me the receipt and a shoebox full of her CDs, a corkscrew from our wine tour in British Columbia, a spare case for her glasses, all of it carrying a faint woodsy smell from his having smoked on the drive over. Something nearly compelled me to ask if he had any pot to share, but instead I asked how the car looked. As he considered this, even the suntan drained out of his face, and behind his patchy goatee I could see the mortified boy. With the shoebox pulled tight to my ribs I lost balance, backed into the nearest wall, and softened down to the carpet.

"Don't go over there," Mark said.

His favor today was coming in early to run the pool heater.

The temperature of the water fluctuates as I tread through, a foot or hand swirling a cool pocket until I've mixed it even, as if it were a baby's bath. I move out to the center of the pool as Charlie, a few feet over me on the board, the glasses back in his hair, stops before the gritty ledge. He pumps his hands and shouts a laugh. His legs bump at the knees. "How come you don't sink?" he says.

I look at the still water around me as my limbs stretch out circles underneath. "This is swimming without going anywhere."

"You look like a turtle-head," he says, venturing less than a step. The board ticks with the small weight of him. Underneath, two coil springs are powdered with chlorine and rust, and spider nests spread from the corners. "You look like Mr. Lizard-head," he says.

"The first time is the hardest. You're okay."

Charlie looks at his feet, his one hand clenching a white fist.

"Trust me," I say, and my treading breaks, a stitch of chlorine in the eyes.

"It's so high."

"It wasn't much lower last time."

"Yes it was. It was too."

"We've got all morning, buddy," I say. "I'm ready when you are." And as I lie back in the womb-like water, I feel something begin to unclench. Layers peel away, the daily routines I'm either doing or psyching myself to do: cooking. Shopping. Facing her family. Facing mine. Suddenly I'm floating without a next thought. And I feel the way you do looking into a canyon, when everything clears from your mind except the impulse to jump.

I catch a wavelet in the mouth and cough it out. My arms slice around until I'm vertical again.

Charlie waits for me and then closes his eyes. "Marco," he says. "Polo."

He looks down at me again. "I might land on your head."

"Let's see you try."

He looks past me to our lounge chairs, and then he pulls the glasses down on his nose. I wonder about the smack of water and if the glasses could hurt him, but the moment is a frail one: he draws his breath and looks like he might do it. He's truly a brave second from stepping off when something happens in the sky. The one low cloud pushes over the sun, and the temperature drops. Bright outlines darken off. Charlie's chest falls, gooseflesh rising on his thighs.

"I'm cold," he says.

"Why don't you throw me those glasses?" I say. "I'll hang on to them until you jump."

"Just wait a minute," he says. "Don't make me, Dad."

The old man passes another lap and Charlie watches. His eyes narrow as if he might call out, interrupt the endless swim, and ask him what? Something it seems Charlie doesn't trust me to answer. But then he looks at me again and stomps his foot. "I hate this. I hate it now." Even as the sun lets go of the cloud and the light comes back, he frowns.

"We'll come back another day," I say, and I twinge with the thought that every next promise for him will be a little easier to break. But we're still in our first year of this. We're still pretty tired.

"I just wish ..." he says and then the tears, big urgent grown-up tears running off. "I just *wish* ..." It's like seeing him cry for the first time, when you wonder how someone so new to life can be so outraged. The glasses slip off his nose, catch on his chin, and in a sudden fit he pitches them down at the water.

Their splash is nothing. They don't float, and my heart catches; I go under. They wobble when I reach for them, and I miss and miss, like grabbing at a butterfly. Looking up I can see my blurry son on the edge of the board, and I send up a hand that just breaks the surface and wave *Don't jump*. I go down after them. They dodge me, they turn and quiver away. And suddenly everything depends on catching these glasses. I howl under water, a puny thing to hear, and then I'm out of air and too far down. I don't know how to swim. I look up and wonder if I'll see him plunge over me in a storm of torpedo bubbles. But there's only the frothy white sky pulling away, and then snow on black in my eyes before the leather hand of God-I-Don't-Believe-In pulls me back.

I sag between the chrome rails of the ladder, belching up water in strings. The old man's voice is airy and rusted. "You're okay," he says. Mark is there, too, gripping my shoulder as to keep me from slipping back. "I thought you guys were just goofing around. Jesus."

"That's never happened before," I say.

"You're okay," the old man repeats, his spongy, arthritic hand on my lower back. And then he says over my head: "He got a swaller in the wrong pipe."

The coughing subsides and my ribs ache. I drop my forehead to my arms, everything slobber and snot, and the old man stays beside me, keeps his hand where it is. In the dark of my piled forearms, I don't want to be let go of.

And where is Charlie? Unexpectedly I trust that he's safe, that I don't have to see. I'll stay here. The fine grit of concrete is warm under my chin. And then Charlie's open little hand is there with the old man's, rubbing, patting me. Under an arm I can see the glasses, a shivering red fleck at the bottom of the pool. "You almost drownded," Charlie says.

I should tell him not to worry, I'm okay, but what I can manage is, "I know." And then the quaking. My knees scrape the side.

"You don't have to get out," he says.

And I nod. I'll stay right here.

Wrench

IN THE MEETINGS THEY TELL YOU TO CELEBRATE YOUR FIRST month, which takes imagination if you never learned how to celebrate sober. Standing in my kitchenette I washed down a thirty-dollar Back to Eden cheesecake with a pint of Sparky's root beer. That same week I soaked a houseplant back to life, filled two vacuum cleaner bags, 409ed the refrigerator, got a haircut, paid some overdraft charges at the bank. I was mindfully tending to the business of day-to-day living. That's something else they tell you.

My Datsun needed repair work in the ballpark of a ground-up restoration, but an oil change was what I could afford. I had it on jack stands in the back lot when I heard the phone up in my apartment.

I was running some furniture and a 27-inch RCA in the *Register Guard* classifieds, and I needed to take the call. It was going on two months since my last paycheck. When Firestone changed hands in the spring they brought in this Apex Tech kid who knew about my drinking, had a stepdad was a big boozer. He fed me no-commission rechecks and started jerking my hours. His RightTrack evaluation called my people skills weak. So one day I loaded up my tools and didn't come back from lunch. I couldn't lay eyes on that kid again. I thought about pouring metal shavings in his motor oil. That's how I used to be.

Instead of a buyer for my TV it was Judy on the line, my ex-wife. We hadn't spoken since I'd been sober. "It feels funny calling you out of the blue," she said, now. "Without provocation, I mean."

Judy's boyfriend Harold brought out the worst in me, incidents of spying, car disabling, late-night engine revving until one of her neighbors got my plate number and turned me in.

"I think it's safe to say you owe me a favor or two," she said.

"I'd do you a favor, Judy. Why wouldn't I?"

She laughed and was quiet. "Harold needed a blow torch to get those potatoes out of his tailpipe. That was you, I know it was."

Harold Moore worked in state corrections up in Salem. To make Friday night happy hour, he'd show up still in his khaki shirt with the steel badge over the pocket. The gang around The Reckloose ate it up, those morons. They came to him for advice, consolation, someone official to feel helpless around. I imagine up in Salem his convicts did too, and Harold distracted them from thoughts of escape or suicide. Same thing at a bar.

"And those hang-ups, after you promised me," Judy said.

I'd had an episode with one of Harold's uniforms the day he moved in with Judy. I was so drunk on so many mixtures I tried to walk myself to the hospital later on.

In the kitchen now, I read a three-by-five card tacked to the wall. STOP-BREATHE-LET GO, it said. My AA sponsor's idea. I had them tacked up by the phone, where I opened mail, where I read the paper.

Judy asked if I could drive her to see about a job on River Road. The cv joint on her Subaru was clicking. She'd taken it in that morning.

"You can blow the axle driving around like that," I said.

She was quiet again, and I read another card. "Good preventative care," I said. "With the car."

"They have twelve forty-five and three-thirty available. I'd prefer earlier, if it's all the same."

"Twelve forty-five it is."

"Are you all right? You sound, I don't know. Perky."

I didn't answer that. Going sober isn't news you share over the phone. She sighed, and I knew there was something coming. "Listen, Lou. If you can't make it, just tell me now."

"I'll make it, Judy. I just said so."

"Because this one's a big deal to me," she said.

*

In the parking lot, someone had made off with my 17mm wrench. I didn't need to double-check my tool box or kick around the weeds, like I would've if I was drinking. There was the railroad tie I'd left it on, right under a goddamn crease in the bumper—when I closed my eyes it was burned there in my memory. I went up to my apartment and paced around the living room. Then I took out a Magic Marker and made a sign.

LOST. ONE MAC 17 MM

CHROME BOX AND OPEN END WRENCH.

APT 9B. REWARD.

I didn't mean the reward part, but what the hell, it wasn't like signing a contract. I taped my sign over the mail cubbies. Then I thought I'd put off the rest of my day and see who answered. When I called Judy and told her what had happened, and to go ahead and take the three-thirty slot, she said, "Jesus Christ. I knew it."

"Just say something came up."

"No, it's fine. I'll tell them I'm changing appointments because my ex-husband is a petty man. There's really something lacking inside you, Lou."

The stairs creaked and I ran to my peephole. Bortnick from 2A stopped midway on the landing, looked at the door across the hall, then down at my wrench in his hand, then at my door.

Bortnick. The guy was like a charter member in the building. His name was in plastic over his mail cubby, while the rest of us had masking tape. A few weeks after my divorce he found me in the dumpster, kicking around for a bottle of Cutty Sark I saw a neighbor throw out on her husband. Bortnick set in a trash bag and noticed the pornography stuck to my ankle. "Talk about spread eagle," he said. "You can just about see what she had for lunch."

"It's not mine," I said, humiliated, sick with a hangover.

Bortnick reached in behind a pizza box, pulled out a five-cent can, polished it on the sleeve of his shirt.

He was panting from the stairs when I opened the door, a short guy with a big gut that went in and out when he breathed. Bigfoot the monster truck on his cap was flattening a Buick.

The Lou I was before AA would've grabbed the wrench and slammed the door. Or better yet, I had these gag twenties a bartender used to pass around, that were just the ends glued together with about an inch missing in the middle. You couldn't tell when they were folded. That and a good beefy handshake is what I'd have given him.

But the Lou I was today stepped back and let him inside.

"I said to myself when I first saw it," he said, handing it over, "that right there's a professional tool." Then he stood by the sofa and looked around my apartment. "I got the same thing downstairs but in reverse. My stove'd be right about over here. Hey. You play that guitar?"

"It's for sale," I said, slipping the wrench in my back pocket. "Matter of fact, I'm taking offers on just about everything you see."

He dropped a hand on the arm of the sofa and rubbed the fabric. He picked up a *Hotrod* from the coffee table and started flipping the pages.

I had a few minutes to kill, so I asked what line of work he was in.

"I work at Goodwill," he said and looked at me as he tossed back the magazine. "Not just retards work there."

"I never said they did."

"You think they let retards do inventorying? That's a good way to go out of business."

I admit that at the dumpster that morning I'd wondered if he was shy a few dots on his dice. But hell, watching me dig under loaded diapers for a bottle of booze, maybe he thought *my* dipstick didn't quite reach the oil.

"It's seizures," he said. "I can fall into a machine or bite off my tongue. You probably heard what happened on the stairs that time." He took off his cap. "Eleven stitches, right across here. They had to put in a new rug. They took it out of my deposit."

He was starting to get on my nerves, now. It was a shame, certainly, but not my fault, and no reason to go around stealing expensive tools. "Recovering isn't any picnic either," I said. "Just think about never being able to go to your own fridge and crack a beer. For the rest of my life, I mean. I can't even make a toast at New Year's."

He shrugged. "You can't drink on Dilantin, either."

I was rubbery now, in a danger zone. Never imagine the rest of your life. I went past him and stood over by the window, where the sun felt strong for early autumn, and leaned my face up on the screen.

I thought about writing him a check and sending him on his way. But then I looked down at my Datsun in the back lot, Old Rusty, its roof paint cracked like a museum piece, and I thought, Nothing doing. The wrench had been right in front of the car, which he'd seen me get out of a hundred times. If he meant to return it, he'd have done it sooner than this.

I corralled him back out the door.

"You don't want to leave tools laying around," he said. "Not in this neighborhood. Just Sunday a guy had his hand cut in front of Two Bit's Worth. Said it was meth heads." He looked at a splotch of paint on his sneaker. He knew what he wanted but couldn't make himself say it.

"Yeah, I heard about that." I twisted the knob and let go. Chut*ching*.

"The thing is, I seen it out in the open. And then I seen your sign. Up at the mail slots."

"Well, I'm the owner. You brought it back to its rightful owner." And I nodded and closed the door.

The house Judy rented was a long, mustard-colored ranch huddled up against other ranches on either side. The only other time I was there was when I set fire to Harold's uniform, and I couldn't remember the layout much, having been obscenely drunk, as I've said.

Judy was waiting for me on the front stoop. She had on a navy blazer with a red blouse, a short pleated skirt also navy, tan pantyhose and heels. She'd bleached her hair, and the color made you notice her mascara and almost green eyes. As she waved and walked over I thought, Jesus. All month I hadn't let myself remember how it used to feel waking up beside her, how I'd show up late to the best job I ever had just to watch her sleep.

In the car she made a comment as she looked up at the bits of foam where a headliner used to be. "Okay, this is nice," is what she said. She set her resume on the ledge of dashboard that wasn't duct taped. "You sure we can make it to River Road in this?" She looked at me and smiled. "I'm kidding, Mr. Sensitive. But for future reference, you should always take the first appointment they offer."

"Sounds like something that pays," I said, keeping it upbeat. I didn't ask what had happened to her job at Motel 6, or why Harold wasn't taking her—I knew he was off today.

"As a matter of fact it's a *pay*roll position. And who's had more money-handling jobs than me?" She went in her purse for cigarettes and pushed the dash lighter. "Now the building is Kinder Associates. It's that Rubik's Cube thing behind the Reckloose."

"I'm on the wagon, Judy. I wanted to tell you. I'm not drinking anymore."

She smiled and lit her cigarette. "Let's not give me a heart attack just now, 'kay Lou? This job is a big deal to me."

"Thirty-four days. I'm just about over the hump."

She shook her head like she knew what would come next. But when she looked at me it wasn't what she'd expected. "Holy shit, you're serious." My ashtray was full of Tootsie Roll wrappers from my sugar cravings, and she flicked her ash out the window. "So. Lou doesn't drink anymore. What does that make me, then?" She put down her visor and looked into a little mirror rubber-banded there.

"It doesn't make you anything," I said.

"I've got this appointment in ten minutes, and now I lose all my confidence." She closed the visor and let out her breath. "No, I'm sorry, Lou. You gave up drinking, and that's wonderful. Really. I'm happy for you." And there was a second, then, when her eyes looked hopeful the way they used to. I mean before I got jealous and could barely hold a conversation without a little fog cutter in my system. Maybe Harold was out of the picture, I thought. Maybe things were finally turning around.

The building was ten stories of chrome glass with "Kinder Associates Incorporated" stamped on a brass plate the size of a windshield. "Give me about twenty minutes," Judy said, touching up her lipstick. I let her out and found a parking spot around back by the dumpsters.

I didn't see Harold Moore's truck in the back of the Reckloose, but that didn't mean he wasn't around, there being baseball on tonight and the Reckloose having the best pregame specials in town. I imagined the cigarette smoke inside and all my ex-friends sitting around in it having conversations. The ring of the tip bell, those handle mugs with little cleated thumb wrests. I looked down at myself, sucked in my gut and made it stay there. I thought about doing a few sit-ups right out on the asphalt.

I was digging "Sweet Judy Blue Eyes" out of my cassettes when Pierce Dwight pulled in with Harold Moore in his passenger seat, causing me to duck over and fiddle with the antenna wire behind the dash.

Doors slammed and Harold said, "Actually, Bruce Lee would mop the floor with Van Damme. No contest at all. Take his one-inch punch. A lot like the phantom punch Ali used on Liston in sixty-five. Only Lee called it the one-inch punch because of how short it travels."

"One-inch punch," Pierce said.

"Did you know he broke a four-ton block of ice in Wisconsin

with that punch?"

"I guess I heard that. Maybe Chuck Norris, then. Hey, what about Norris, Harold?"

And then there was bar music when the door opened, and I didn't hear anything else.

When Judy came out I was parked at the curb facing Chambers Street. I was just sitting there wondering about the strange vacuum in my chest. I didn't want to hate Harold anymore, and hatred had been taking up room. My sponsor said that animosity and vengeance are siren songs for my personality type. I remembered an AA story where a guy hung up on his brother-in-law, and next thing he knew he was on his fourth Manhattan in a bar he'd never set foot in before. It was like the aliens beamed him up, he said.

Judy closed her door so hard the window crank fell off. She pinched the bridge of her nose. "Can we just go somewhere?" she said.

"We'll stop at Chauncey's," I said. "I'm buying. I'll get a soda."

Judy drew back from her fingers and shook her head, smiling. "No, we won't. Let's just pretend I never said that."

First gear resisted the shifter with the sound of an automatic pencil sharpener. I shut the engine off, found first, restarted, all the while looking up at the Kinder Associates building. Its windows reflected a short lawn so green it was blue, along with a string of azaleas cut like ice cubes. The bark mulch was the new kind they spray-paint red to look more natural.

"It doesn't look like your kind of place at all," I said.

"Not even in the ballpark. I mean, I would've turned down keys to the executive toilet, you know? They could offer me vice president, for all I care now."

On the Beltline we got caught in the four o'clock bottleneck at Delta Highway. We came to a stop just over the Willamette River, where a line of retired men were fishing for summer steelhead. To the east, the Coburg hills had been clear cut, and the blond patches were just waiting for a freight train spark to light everything up.

"Even with a resume you have to fill out their application," Judy was saying. "And then you need a Ph.D in rocket science for some nine-dollar filing job."

"And then you're *over* qualified," I said. In a friendly way I reached over and squeezed her thigh, not putting the moves on, but just to say to hell with the world and everyone in it. But her face changed, and I took my hand back. "Let's forget about this day all together," she said.

Outside the car window on Judy's side, one of the old men hooked a fish, probably a late spring chinook by the way his pole doubled over. The other men pulled in their lines, and one of them waded out with a net.

"I lied to you once already today," Judy said, watching the commotion. "My car's at the shop because Wednesday I rear-ended an old man in a brown Escort. His little car, Lou—my God—glass was all over the place and the fender came off. I swear I thought, 'That's it, Judy. You finally killed somebody.'" She laughed in a way that seemed to keep her from crying. "He was meeting his wife for lunch at Wendy's. I was almost the end of sixty-one years of marriage."

"Wow," I said. It was all I could think of.

"It was the day I quit working for that son of a bitch Roy. You know what he did? I caught him behind the front desk peeping on a couple in room 2. He drilled a hole behind the calendar. Oh, I was so mad. I always knew there was a slitheriness to that man, and I'd always put it out of my mind. But when I caught him with that hole it was just the end of my rope. Like I never do any good, I never *act*. And then I turned off Kellogg and had my accident. I try to do the decent thing and look what happens."

"Wait a minute, Judy."

"And you know the worst part? I was talking to Mr. Seifret—the man I hit—waiting for the cops, and everything about him suddenly made me jealous. I wanted sixty-one years with somebody. I wanted great-granddaughters. Your problem is you never took the time to find out what I wanted."

"And your problem is you over-analyze every other goddamn thing. Think simple, Judy. It was a car wreck, that's all."

When I looked at her she smirked like she'd just proven her point. "Think simple," she said. "Stick it to him before he sticks it to you. Isn't that your motto?"

"Okay. Here we go. Everything's my fault, now." I swerved out of traffic and broken divider lines shot under the front end.

Judy's driveway was spotted with oil from Harold's GMC, but you couldn't tell how old the spots were. I parked in front of her garage door and flipped the key back. Judy was trying to open the passenger door. "Is this goodbye?" I said.

"It's whatever you want it to be." She got the door opened, and I came around and followed up to the house. Inside she dropped her purse on a mica table and kicked off her heels. "I'm having a drink now," she said, "because my day's been reductive. But your ID isn't any good around here, I'm afraid."

"Is there root beer?"

Judy laughed. Then she looked at me in a way that reminded me of the time I had a cold and she came home early from work with NyQuil and Chunky soup. I was in my pajamas on the couch watching *The Jetsons*, and Judy stopped and leaned on the doorjamb, her arms full of paper bags. It was that same kind of look now, as if she were seeing the most innocent thing in the world. "No, I'm sure there's no root beer," she said. "But let's see what I can find."

When she was gone I looked in the fire place, which was clean, no Duraflame log like the one I'd used to burn up Harold's uniform, and no more ashes. It seemed like a good sign. Our old sofa sat against the opposite wall, a corduroy sectional from the eighties. Her Adidas were by the coffee table, her Ansel Adams print over the TV. And the Oregon Ducks cap could have been Judy's. Sure. Why not? She used to wear them. My day-off look, she used to say.

I heard the suction sound of a freezer door. "You're not snooping out there, are you?" she said. "It makes me nervous when you get quiet."

Her computer was set up in the dining area. On the glass table were more copies of her resume, each different in some way, her Special Skills listed first on one, third down on the next, her name and address centered and then on the left margin. More of the same paper was balled up in the trash basket.

"I've been different this past month, Judy. I know what that sounds like."

"In what way?" she said.

"Recovering. It changes a person."

"That's sort of a religious commitment, right? That whole twelve-step thing?"

I heard her set a glass on the counter, and then the bottle. I could tell she was trying to pour quietly.

"It's not so bad," I said. "They get a verse in here and there, but it's just the old knee-benders that use them all. The rest of us pick and choose the everyday steps, like deflating your ego." I was about to get comfortable on the sofa when I spotted something through the cracked door of the bedroom.

"And you think it's what you'll stick with down the road?"

"You know what it feels like, Judy? Taking karate when I was thirteen. Only I get to a new belt every month I'm sober."

For a few seconds the kitchen was quiet. Then she said, "I'm proud of you, Lou."

I pictured how her eyes would be when I walked in, and what that moment might produce. But then I turned and went into the bedroom. Spread over the foot of the bed was Harold's khaki uniform shirt, still on a hanger.

Judy was there in the doorway as I came out of her bathroom.

I'd been in the cabinet under the sink. Clenched in my hands were such liquids as to clean, shine and disinfect the shirt into oblivion.

"I think you just demoted yourself to white belt," Judy said. She came in and set her vodka and an iced tea for me on the nightstand.

"What's this?"

"What does it look like? You burned one up, remember?"

"You said he moved out."

"I never said that. You just invent your own personal version of everything. If it's any of your business, Harold only visits now. He just didn't get all his stuff."

"But you're still..." I made a kissy face.

"God, would you grow up?"

"Well, good. That's fine," I said. "I think that's just perfect." I stared at her glass on the nightstand. Something was going to happen, that was clear. When it came down to it, all the power words they give you fall flat, and it's just you and your days sober. Thirty-four days. That's what I said to myself looking at that vodka. That was the face Judy was seeing when she said, "Lou," and her voice fell soft. "I think you'd better go now, Lou."

I dropped the cleaning bottles and picked up the khaki shirt by the throat. I shook it and collapsed the wire hanger in my fist.

"Put that down right now," Judy said, sounding like, well, like a woman who'd lived with me for five years. I dropped it on the bed, and she gathered up the Windex and Lysol and Ty-D-Bol. "Lou gets his feelings hurt and goes on a rampage," she said. "Why is that song familiar?"

I went to the window and pulled a gap down in the blinds, though they were open and I could see all of Market Street. But that's what you do when your pulse is hammering in your throat. You pull down a gap in the blinds.

"Harold talks to me," she said. "I'm not ashamed of him. He believes in me. And you know what he doesn't do? He never acts like there's something wrong with me. You couldn't even talk to me, you couldn't even…make love unless you were drunk. How do you think that made me feel?"

Judy was waiting for an answer when I finally turned around. Her eyes weren't green anymore but blue with the afternoon light, and small because she was angry, and glassed because she was sad.

"I guess what's the point?" I said. "You have Harold now. You two are a match made in heaven, from what I understand."

"Goddamn you, Lou. You'll never change. You know what you should be worried about right now? You should be thinking why not you, why not us. I never would've married you if I thought for a second I'd want to leave you. I wanted to be old-fashioned. *I* wanted great-granddaughters." She pressed her temples and paced the length of the bed. "And there was a time, I know I'm not imagining it, when we used to be partners. I don't know what happened. And now *you're* not even drinking anymore. God, I could scream. Here you are sober and I can't even get a job filing papers."

"Judy, look," I said. And what I wanted to say, finally, was how afraid I always was of losing her, how in my dreams I kept losing her to someone better. But then a shiver came over me and I just stared at the vacuum lines in the carpet. Judy was taking a drink when I looked back. She said, "Mm-mm" when our eyes met and walked into the bathroom. She spit out the vodka and poured what was left down the drain. Then she came back and folded over the corner of the bed, tucked her feet between the sheets and lay back on the pillow. She seemed to be going to sleep right there, in broad daylight. Maybe a minute passed before she rolled forward and looked at me. "Well?" she said, and I saw that it was too late to say anything. "Can we say you've put the exclamation point on the end of my day?"

I parked behind my building and just slumped there awhile on the steering wheel. Who should I have passed on Mohawk Avenue but

Bortnick carrying two paper sacks from Winco. When I looked up again he was on the back landing, stabbing his hand around for the doorknob. I got out and slammed the car door. Bortnick swung around, and a giant bag of M&M's tipped out of one of the sacks. It split on the ground and little candies wobbled all over the back stoop. Bortnick bent forward and set his bags down.

"That's a shitload of M&M's," I said. "Where'd you have to go? The factory?"

He pointed at a bag to say he'd bought them at Winco. Then he knelt down and started dropping candies back into the torn bag.

"Just clear me a path to get in," I said.

He kept pinching them off the concrete in his fat fingers.

"Hell, man," I said. "Kick them into the grass, will you? Something'll come along and eat them. Use your head."

But Bortnick just kept getting them one at a time, and when there was enough room for my foot I stepped over him and opened the door.

"Thanks for making us miss that first appointment," I said. "You know what I want right now more than a million dollars? A goddamn drink is what I want. Thank you." But he was miles away in the shade of his hat brim.

On the stairs to my apartment I stopped three times, once to forget about Bortnick, once to forget Harold, and a last time to remember something that had happened years before in a house in Junction City. It was a few weeks into the New Year, and I was playing my guitar. I had a fire going in the little fireplace behind me, and my back was itchy with the kind of heat that's a luxury when you know how cold and wet it is outside. Judy came out of the kitchen with a spatula in one hand and a plate in the other, and she said, "That's it, Lou. That kind of sound is just what I mean." She told me that what I had was the real deal, that she believed in me. She'd come out in the middle of flipping a burger onto a bun.

Then I discovered that with the commotion I'd left my keys

down in the ignition. Bortnick was still there when I came down, still picking up candy off the stoop. I could hear the little things he was whispering. He was counting them. He was counting all that goddamn candy.

"Those aren't any good, now," I said. "What are you doing? Hey."

But he kept picking them up, one at a time, and dropping them into the torn bag.

"Listen, do you know what some of these people track in on their shoes? Meyers in 4A, he's a butcher, for God's sake. Think of what he's walking in all day."

I sat on the second step. I picked an M&M and ate it. I ate several at a time. "Now you can't count them," I said. "You don't know how many that was."

His face was squashy like a water balloon from bending over. "They're for a raffle where I work," he said. "I was supposed to get at least five hundred."

I scooped up a handful. A sugar craving may have been all it was, but somehow these were the best M&M's I'd ever tasted. "You know," I said, in between chews, "it is entirely possible to head back to that same store and buy yourself another bag."

Bortnick looked down at the dirty stoop. The sun was over the building, and the candies, especially the dark ones, were getting hard to see. He put one hand against the edge of the step and plowed a bunch of them across with the blade of the other hand. Then he turned around and sat beside me. He giggled. He had the kind of laugh you could feed forever. His eyebrows spread apart. He said, "Let Sandra buy her own raffle candy." One at a time he started popping them in his mouth.

We kept eating. "To hell with Sandra," I said. I kept shoveling them in. I could have knocked off every last one. "We're sorry, Sandra," I said, candy shell rattling around my tongue, "but we pigged out on your raffle. We gorged. We had a feast."

Backlash

Eric Hill was in the west wing boys room when Mickey Anderson came in to use the other urinal. The hall pass in his teeth Eric inched to the side, trying painfully to finish. Anderson had been a year ahead of Eric and probably didn't know who he was, but as Eric stared at the cinderblock wall—in black Sharpie: Dave Tanner ~~sucks rules~~ is dead meat—he could only imagine getting his ass kicked in the empty bathroom, middle of fourth period.

Through the rest of Social Studies he wondered how fast Anderson was, what he could bench, if the two guys Eric had taken in fights could take Anderson. A montage of wild hooks and undercuts, bloody mouths and choke holds, ran through his mind as Mr. Zimmerman droned on like a faraway chainsaw about the Berlin Wall coming down.

Eric and Heather skipped fifth period like they did every Friday. In his El Camino Heather smoked quietly, stubbornly it seemed, as Eric kept gunning the engine and then riding the brakes into curves. He meant to keep his mouth shut until she confessed something. Anderson, before dropping out last winter, had told it around school that he had dumped Heather, but Eric believed Heather's version, especially about what a mistake Anderson had been. If Anderson had come to see her, why wouldn't she say something? What was she trying to hide?

He watched her push in the dashboard lighter. "You just got done with one," he said.

She cracked her window. "Can you slow down please?"

"I didn't know if anything's wrong."

"Is it a capital crime to have another cigarette?"

Up ahead a logging truck was chugging pecker poles, and Eric dropped the pedal to pass on a stretch of Hayhurst that was solid-lined but should have been dashed. It was fine until the wet road sent them into a fish tail he barely pulled out of, and Eric knew that his chances of getting Heather to admit anything were lost.

Friday was their day to fool around before his mother got home. On his bed they'd eat Lucky Charms and watch *The Bugs and Woody Hour*, she'd take out her ponytail, and by the time *He-Man* came on they'd be making out, Eric on his back kissing her in the electric, fruity-smelling cavern of her hair. Always he'd ease his fingers into the elastic of her panties, and always she'd find his hand and say, "We should stop," and then they would.

He didn't know if any of that was salvageable now, Heather still fuming, but as he swung into his driveway a new problem suddenly outweighed his concern. Parked in front of the garage door was a boxy white F-100, beside which Eric's father stood holding a fishing rod on the front lawn.

Eric slammed the steering wheel. "Jesus Christ."

"Is that him?" Heather said.

Eric looked up through the windshield, blinking off the burn in his eyes.

"It's fine," Heather said. "You're being weird, anyway."

Realizing they were about to lose their Friday together, Eric turned to her and said, "When are we ever going to get to be intimate together. I just want to know."

She tried to laugh, but he saw the redness on her throat, the deep oblong blush as if being upset embarrassed her. "Do you even know what intimate means? It's not the same thing as sex."

"Sometimes it is."

"I have to pee, and then I'm walking home." She took his keys out of the ignition. "At least go say something to him," she said, and then went in the house through the garage.

Eric waited a long minute before he got out of the car. Frank, his father, was reeling line onto a salmon rod. "I remember when you used to hold my spools on a pencil," Frank said. "I had to get it all on before you counted Mississippis up to fifty, remember?"

Eric stared at the spool hopping around the grass clippings. It had been since Christmas that they'd seen each other, and with gritty silence Eric made his resentment clear. He looked up at his father with narrowed eyes, a flat mouth. He felt sure he finally outweighed Frank, who was still just as lean in his Costco jeans and Oregon Ducks sweatshirt as when he used to ride around on a mountain bike visiting his congregation. He was fifty, just about fifty.

Frank continued reeling until the last of the line brought the spool off the ground. "My sources tell me the springers are in at Lake Creek," he said. "And they're thick this year."

"You're supposed to call before you come over," Eric said.

"This seemed to be extenuating—"

"Did you go by my school first?"

Frank's look became serious as he turned down his eyes. He set his rod against the truck fender. "I didn't, no."

"Call if you want to see me," Eric said. "I mean it."

"Eric, what is your problem today?" Heather said. She'd come out quietly and was in the driveway now with her backpack on. "He's in some kind of mood, Mr. Hill," she said. "I'm Heather."

Frank shook hands with Heather as Eric watched with alarm. He assumed Heather knew what everyone else did about his father (he'd scratched out graffiti and almost gotten in a fist fights over Frank), but he'd never imagined letting Heather actually meet him.

Heather must've asked about the salmon rod. When Eric could focus on listening he heard Frank describing the spring Chinook run on the Siuslaw.

"Is that trout?" Heather said.

"Salmon. They're really something to see. I'd love if you joined us."

"Thank you, but sorry," she said to Frank. "I don't fish."

"You said you wanted to learn," Eric said. A puddle of heat had spread in his stomach with the realization that they were having their first fight. If she left him now it seemed very possible that it would be for good. "It quit raining," he said and lifted his eyes skyward. But when he looked at her again Heather wore an expression that said the next word out of his mouth better be the right one. "Please," he said.

On the twenty-minute drive into Eugene, the three of them side-by-side on Frank's bench seat, Heather talked with Frank as though Eric wasn't even there. She asked him if he was still a pastor up in Portland.

"Oh, no," Frank said, "Heavens, no. I think it's safe to say I've worn out my welcome with the Bishop." He didn't act ashamed or guilty, and then he went on about his new state job picking up leftover restaurant food for soup kitchens, which Heather thought was wonderful. At one point she seemed so agreeable that Eric reached over and took her hand, but she stared ahead at the cars on the interstate, her fingers cool and limp. After he finally let go she drew the hand back to her lap.

GI Joes in Eugene had canoes and dome tents hanging from the ceiling. Eric and Heather followed Frank to the fishing aisle, which Eric knew well from the time he was nine and they moved west from Emmett, Idaho, until he was fourteen, when his father ruined his life. It was only two years ago, but it was all of Eric's high school so far.

The man who printed their salmon tags kept doubling up the computer keys with his thick fingers. He had the powerful, barrel-chested build of an out-of-work logger. Spotted owl protection had closed down mills all over the place, and you saw them greeting and stocking shelves and pumping gas. "Shittin' thing," he said as the register blared and beeped.

Heather was staring at the big salmon mounted over a

mannequin in chest waders. Eric was about to teach her how to identify a Chinook from a Coho by its dark mouth when the counterman noticed her and said, "It ain't real. They got a place up in Canada makes them out of plastic." He glanced back at the fish. "I caught a couple like it before. Bright as a nickel, too."

"That must be a fifty-pound fish," Frank said.

As Eric started filling in his height and weight on the license, the sound of Frank's voice in conversation reminded him of Sunday night dinners at the parsonage. The company was usually housewives with their mill worker husbands, big dangerous-looking men who called his father reverend. Eric felt a sudden nostalgia for those nights, and it made him bitter.

"How's school?" Frank said as Eric handed the counterman his information. Frank had lined up twenty or so corkies—pea-sized wooden balls—on the glass counter. They were glossy variations of pink and red, some swirled, some with glitter.

"Why didn't you get any blue ones?" Eric said. "Or black?"

"They can't see dark in high water," the counter man said.

Frank pressed his lips and sighed. "He knows that," he said.

"School's not bad," Eric said as the counterman looked from Frank to Eric to Frank again and then went back to get plastic wallets for the tags.

Across the aisle Heather was pushing through a rack of fleece vests. Eric watched her hold up a powder blue one that matched her eyes and saw a guy with sunglasses back in his hair check her out from the camping aisle. She caught him and he smiled until she looked away.

Eric watched the landscape rushing past as they approached the coastal range. Highway 126 was lined with slender third-growth trees, and the dark under their crowded boughs was the dark of night. Occasionally the trees thinned around a trailer or small frame house, and in a field brown and white cows were standing around near the road. Their mop-head tails slapped their flanks behind the ribs, and then the big dumb faces with far-apart eyes and noses like footballs would swivel back and lash a foamy tongue at flies the tails had missed.

"My uncle caught a burnt salmon a few weeks ago," Heather was saying. "I think that's what he called it, burnt."

"It means it was ready to die," Frank said. "It's like they have fuses. As soon as they hit the fresh water they start to fall apart. You can hook a fish in the Willamette that's already gone two hundred miles."

"Just to mate?"

"Just to lay eggs, or fertilize them. They never actually touch each other."

Twice, Eric came close to breaking his silence. He resented not being the one to teach Heather salmon, their runs, the snowmelt hitting the river mouth where they waited, signaling that water levels were right; or that they bit at roe not for nourishment but survival of the fittest; or where the fin is clipped off on hatchery fish—the only fish you're allowed to keep.

"Are the fish burnt where we're going?" Heather said.

"These are chromers. They ought to be as bright as that one up in the store."

Eric opened the triangle vent window, and a loud, obnoxious wind shot through the cab. "I'd never buy a Ford," he said, loudly over the whistling. "You want to break in, all you need is a popsicle stick to flip up this latch. And just about any Ford key will start any other Ford." He closed the window.

"One of my mother's friends still goes to Trinity," Heather said to Frank. "She thought it was awful how they treated you. So many people here are old-fashioned."

"He's the reason I'm not a Christian anymore," Eric said.

"That's not true," Heather said without looking at him. "He thinks church is full of hypocrites."

"Starting with him," Eric said. Watching out his window,

he could feel Heather's stare, like an open flame near his cheek. "How's your boyfriend?" Eric said to Frank. "He still a nurse?"

"He's fine, and yes he is. I'll tell him you were asking."

"No, don't bother."

"Eric, can we be ..." Frank opened and closed his hands on the steering wheel. "Enough is enough," he said.

"He won't admit it," Heather said, "but I think he really misses you."

"Jesus Christ," Eric said. He rolled down his window to spit.

Any minute now the Siuslaw River would come into view. Eric didn't remember quite where it happened, but he could feel the old anticipation building. The largest salmon he'd ever caught weighed almost thirty pounds—he was twelve and landing that fish by himself was probably the greatest accomplishment of his life so far.

"I wish people would just mind their own business," Heather said to Frank.

"God bless it, Heather, Cottage Grove isn't the most progressive community in the world. You're an exception, I can tell already."

"I mean, okay, maybe being gay is a sin, but what about the million other ones? You're not supposed to eat pork, right? Yet everyone eats bacon."

"We're nothing if not judgmental." Frank went on to tell about the hate mail, the hang-ups in the middle of the night, even when they wrote "Queer" on the parsonage lawn with gasoline. It sickened Eric that he couldn't even figure out a way to interrupt without sounding like a jerk.

"Okay, so in your opinion, who gets into heaven?" Heather said.

"In my opinion everyone gets there."

"Lucky for you," Eric said, and they both ignored him.

"Then which commandments are the worst to break, I guess I mean. Which forbid you automatically from going to heaven?"

Frank laughed quietly. "Heather, I think if we love each other, we're all getting in. If we're committed to each other. Jesus never mentions homosexuality per se, but what he does object to is divorce. We shouldn't divorce each other. That's what I regret most, divorcing Peg and moving away from my family. It was complicated. It's still complicated."

"But if somebody did something really awful." Heather cut herself off, opening her purse. "Mr. Hill, do you think I could smoke in here?"

Frank leaned forward and pulled open the ashtray. "You go right ahead."

The Siuslaw was under them now, down a ravine off Eric's side of the truck. He could see it shimmering between the small firs, and drift boats were anchored above the chutes where salmon stacked up in holding lies to run the whitewater.

Heather lit her cigarette and for a while didn't say anything. Then she said, "I guess it's hard to think of God forgiving anything. I mean, anything."

"Think of what God forgives in the Old Testament. David alone." Frank was grinning as he glanced at Heather, and the grin fell away.

"What about abortion?" she said. "That's killing. How could God ever possibly forgive that?" She was almost shouting, and Eric stared at her without knowing what to feel or what to show that he was feeling. Her eyes reddened and she pulled short drags from her cigarette. "That's killing," she said, again. "I'm a killer."

"Honey," Frank said, "no, no. Didn't they counsel you? What did they say?"

"How isn't it killing?"

"I can tell you're a good person, Heather," Frank said, and very easily, as he drove, he put his arm around her. Hugging for him always came easily. He said that we're often called to look beyond scripture. How we are destined to make mistakes and how unequivocal God's love and forgiveness is and, again, how she was a good person.

They passed the quarter-mile sign for the Upper Siuslaw Boat Launch, and Frank began letting off on the gas and turned on his signal light. As he was talking, he looked at Eric. It was a serious, expectant look that assumed Eric was the one who had gotten her pregnant, and Eric waited to see disappointment surface on his father's face. He geared himself for the prospect of telling his father he lost his right to judge anyone ever again. But the look never came.

"I like to stop here," Frank told Heather, a little awkward now, after he'd parked the truck, "and take a look at the rigs they're tying." He smiled. "Fishing's better up where we're going, but the folks up there pretend it isn't." The engine ticked cool as they stared at towering limbless trunks and the sudden shimmer of water behind them.

Eric felt dizzy. He couldn't push from his mind the idea of Anderson having sex with Heather. When his father was gone, Eric felt strangely afraid of Heather's choppy, after-crying breaths. He stared out the windshield. The building was a lean-to structure of rough-hewn cedar with a shaker roof. A sign on the back of it read NATIVE FISH MUST BE RELEASED UNHARMED.

"Even the salmon," Heather was saying softly. "All they go through for their babies."

"That's why Anderson was at school today?" Eric said.

"He says I owe him half the money. He just wants to be a jerk because he hates me. He said he'd tell everyone if I don't pay him."

A taste rose in his mouth, and suddenly Eric punched the dashboard as hard as he could sitting down. He hit it again. "Stop, Eric!" Heather yelled. The vinyl cracked and behind it the tan foam was dented three times from his knuckles. He jerked back and dropped an undercut to the glove box, creasing the metal before the door fell open. Heather screamed. Her cigarette fell as she pressed both hands against her eyes.

Eric sat back panting and watched the cigarette on her thigh. He was too pumped up to do anything about it, and suddenly she cried out and swatted it away. It left a smear of gray ash on her jeans and had burned her. As he realized this, something loosened inside. He watched his forearm where two veins surfaced like cables. And for what seemed a long time they sat there not talking. He'd never seen Heather cry before, and now he'd seen it twice in ten minutes.

She held her hands over her face, and Eric looked at the beat-up dashboard. Only then did his right hand start to hurt. He turned over the two bloody knuckles and pressed them into his pants.

"It's called a plunking shack," he said, staring at the three-walled structure. Heather lowered her hands and sat blinking. "To sit in when it rains. You put on four ounces of lead and drop some roe out in a boil, then stick the rod butt in a pipe. Some guys clothespin a little bell on so they don't have to watch it."

"He wouldn't even go in the clinic with me," she said. "He just took off somewhere. When it was over I had to wait for an hour and a half sitting on the curb." She shook her head, and he watched her mouth tighten and frown and shake.

"That son of a bitch."

"I didn't want you to ever know about it. I wanted us to be … I wanted everything to just be normal. I wanted us to be in love."

The word passed through him and left him hazy.

"When it happens for us, it'll just happen," she said. "I can't tell you when."

Eric looked out at the pavement to the boat launch, where old leaves were plastered like cereal mush. He sighed and felt his shoulders drop.

"Don't ever call it doing the deed," she said. "Mickey used to say that. I hate that."

"I won't," Eric said.

Frank appeared from behind the plunking shack and started up toward the truck. There were those in his church who would go to the clinics with signs and pictures of dead fetuses. The few times he mentioned these people, Frank neither approved nor disapproved of what they were doing. He prayed for them. He prayed even for the people who were hateful at the end. It never seemed to do any good, but Eric believed that his father was saying a prayer for Heather now, and he found comfort in that.

When Frank opened the driver's door Eric looked up and smiled.

Frank took off his sunglasses. "What did you do?" he said, looking at the dashboard. "Eric. Answer me."

Eric reached forward and tried to close the glove box. It stayed on the third try. "I'll pay to get it fixed," he said.

"You're damn right, you're going to pay for it," Frank said. "I don't believe you." He leaned back out of the truck and looked down at the river. "What do I do here?" he said. Heather took Eric's hand and brought it close to her.

Frank looked back inside the truck.

"He was just …" Heather said. "He's okay now, Mr. Hill. We're both okay."

Frank went around to the front of the truck and leaned against the grille, craned his head back and stretched his neck from side to side. Eric got out and helped Heather out his door, and they came around to stand with him.

Facing the hood of the truck now, Frank closed his eyes a moment. "You've still got a lot of growing up to do. I see that now."

This hurt to hear, but Eric swallowed and kept quiet.

"If you don't like your life," his father said, "then you can blame me for it. You can blame God or whoever you want."

"I said I'll pay for it," Eric said, staring down at his untied Timberlands.

"And I'm asking you what then, son? Look at me."

But by the time Eric looked up, it was too late. His father was staring at the hood of the truck, against which his hands were pressed, arms stiff.

"I don't know what made me do that," Eric said. "Look, okay? I'm sorry. But we want to fish. Let's just go fishing, Dad."

Carrying his father's tackle box, big as a microwave, Eric spotted crayfish on the submerged volcanic stone of the run-off basins. Their loud red lobster bodies looked as alien to this place as the bright lures hanging from the maple branches over the water.

Near the popular holes they had to watch their step around cans and bottles and empty tackle packages, some of it burned or melted in fire pits. Bank fishermen bounced lead through every reachable chute and boil. Running yarn-trimmed corkies they tossed out over each other at forty-five degrees, timed as if they were geared to a common sprocket, until the call "Fish on!" obliged all but the lucky one to haul in their lines.

It was hard not to stay and watch the big fish landed, but Frank wanted to find a hole that wasn't getting quite as hammered. The path wound down to the waterline, and every few minutes would come a horrible murky smell. Heather was the first to say something, and Eric pointed to a rotting salmon carcass half up the bank. There was a brown head and white ribs down to the tail, which was whole and still in the water.

On an egg-shaped bank of sand Eric put together Heather's rod, wet the line and tied the swivel with a clinch knot as his father talked with the next man upriver. The water had that greenish color you wanted, between the clarity of low water, when fish are easily spooked, and the brown boil of heavy rain and melt-off. Within casting distance upstream the river slowed into a pocket where salmon would likely stack up before running the chute.

Eric cautioned Heather about backlash with the bait-casting reel as he threw a few light casts in demonstration. When it was her turn she swatted forward the way you can with an open-faced reel, and the bird nest was considerable. He had to cut out some line. On her next cast the backlash wasn't quite so bad.

"Maybe you should just fish," Heather said. "I keep screwing up."

"You're okay," he said. He picked out the snags and took in the slack, holding the line taut with a finger. He stood behind Heather and positioned her hands. "Imagine there's a ball of whipped cream on the tip of the rod," Eric said, his father's trick. "You want to just lob it out there."

Heather cast again, and this time all it took was a little tug at two of the loops and the current pulled out the slack. "I still didn't get it out very far," she said.

"You're doing fine," his father said behind them. Even less backlash the next cast, and then she sailed the weight out thirty feet and didn't tangle at all. Eric moved up against her as she waved the rod tip over the water, following the taut line through the current. He rubbed the skin above her elbows. He thought about her with a baby inside and waited for an emotion to come to him, and when it did he lifted her hair off her collar and kissed the warm back of her neck. "Hey," she whispered, though she didn't pull away.

He laced his hands over the taut skin of her belly. His life had never come to him with such clarity as it did right then.

An enormous platinum salmon jumped a riffle upstream. It appeared all at once over the current, head and tail full out—more artificial-looking in its suspension than the one at the store—then dropped belly-first into a slick of bubbled water. "That *whale*?" Heather said. "Is that what I'm trying to catch?"

Eric went up the bank to tie a rig for himself. He met his father at the tackle box and started putting a rod together. Frank passed Eric a corky with a swirl of pastel colors. "Raspberry sherbet. The secret weapon."

Eric took the little ball and threaded it onto his leader line.

"She's a beautiful young woman," his father said.

Eric thought to say that the baby wasn't his, but when he looked up at his father knotting his hook, the impulse to tell him everything didn't come. "When we get back to the house," Eric said, "are you going to come in and see Mom?"

Frank pulled the tag end of the knot with his teeth. "You think she'd want me to?"

Suddenly Heather screamed, "Guys. Hey guys," and when Eric turned back she was pulling hard, everyone around her hauling in their lines. His father rushed down. Heather tugged again and then just handed him the rod. Holding it bent over his head, Frank waited for the pull of life on the other end, and Eric remembered passing his father a rod that first time, when he knew the fish was big, one that could pull you in, but he'd hooked it, he'd hooked a monster, and here, Dad, take it, Dad, I need you. His father held the rod high and didn't move, didn't breathe, and closed his eyes.

Now when he opened them a look of peace settled on his face, and he lowered the rod, the bend coming out of it, the lead caught on a root or some tangled line, and he smiled gently at Heather before he leaned toward her and broke her heart.

Wild Life

RONNIE LOGAN SHOT ME WITH THE TWELVE-GAUGE, AND THEN ran down through the birch trees yelling, "You're fine! You're fine!" Out of breath he patted my back, shook my hand, gave me a pocket-warm stick of Hubba Bubba. "Here," he said, shoving the gun at me. "Keep it. It used to be my dad's."

Most of the pellets had blown apart a rotten stump I'd had my foot on. My Van Halen shirt was peppered with tree crumbs. Pellets had gone into my leg under the knee, more than one but I couldn't tell how many more. I looked at the gun. "Walter Stuckey gave you that for your go-kart. I was there."

"You were moving around like a buck," he said.

"I was standing still."

He wiped his forehead with his thermal sleeve.

"We're hunting pheasant, " I said.

"It's dark in here. I can't even see."

The pellets stung like nettles and began to ooze. Suddenly I wanted no more guns, and I threw down my single-shot twenty-two. "Leave yours, too," I said. Ronnie's eyes narrowed to slits and he chewed a thumbnail. He was eighteen and I was fifteen. When he was ten a Sunshine Dairy truck knocked him off his bike, and now he had gran mals about once a month and couldn't pass freshman math. In times of crisis Ronnie trusted me to know what to do. He dropped the rusty Remington in the leaves and got his neck and shoulder under my arm. After a while he led us out of the shaggy little white-barked trees. We'd been hunting since dawn, and my camo pants were stiff and heavy with dew, scuffing my shins like cardboard. As we entered a field he flattened his lips and spat in the high clover. "You telling your mom?" he said.

"Let me shoot you and see what you do."

It was our first summer as friends. I'd been staying at his house three and four nights a week since school let out, and already we were Peppermint Schnapps alcoholics and Tiparillo inhalers. Around bon-fires we'd inventory an old stock tank full of stolen mailboxes, throwing knives, license plates, Vietnamese porn, half a gallon of pure grain, and three sticks of ammonia gelatin dynamite. We were just about third-world civil war kids running around. It wasn't surprising at all that a thing like this had happened.

We hobbled between fields along a poplar shelterbelt, and soon the first tattered outbuildings of the Logan dairy rose into view. Ronnie's father had died of a heart attack in the stanchion barn three years before, and now the old timothy fields were choked with cocklebur and poison ivy, the manure pile waist-high in saplings. His mother stayed in the farmhouse with her box wine and emphysema. Once in a while she'd appear in the living room, stooped and yellowed and coughing horrifically, and I'd stare at the TV until she passed on through to the kitchen.

Ronnie had three fat older sisters we feared and hated, but some of their friends who slept over were only ten or so pounds from pretty. When our bon fires died out and the dew was on us like a sneeze from God, we'd come inside to find them sleeping on sofas in front of *Get Smart* or *Bewitched* or *My Three Sons*. We'd steal change and cigarettes out of their purses. We'd touch their forearms with our tongues and put one girl's hand across another girl's thigh.

Suddenly Ronnie stopped on the trail and shushed me. Someone up ahead was yelling, a raspy cigarette voice coming from the property next to his. He dragged me across the driveway to where Mrs. Feiner, our school bus driver, was hanging out of a sash window on the back of the house. The window brace had broken, and she was trying to pull the air conditioner unit back in by its louvered sides. Ronnie plopped me down on in the gravel and got under the unit, heaving it up near the window. Mrs. Feiner drew her hands back. "I barely touched the stupid thing," she said.

Maura, her daughter, came out the back door and got the cord where it was pinched in the splintered windowsill. She backed away as Ronnie lowered the air conditioner to the ground, and then turned and saw me. I was used to short glances of boredom or disdain from girls my age, but Maureen saw my pain and covered her mouth. "I got shot in the leg," I said.

"Oh, God."

"It's Dale Mazik, from school," Ronnie said. Maura came over and helped me up. She must've just come from the shower; her face glistened and her damp hair smelled like apples. Her blouse had elastic cinched around over her breasts, which, since the last time I'd seen her—before she dropped out of school in the fall—had doubled in size.

Mrs. Feiner came around and held open the back door. She had bright yellow hair that feathered off the sides and a made-up face guys fantasized about in that long school-bus mirror over the windshield. On her waitress blouse was a Beefsteak Charlie's nametag that said *HELEN* and *How do you take your steak?*

She shook out a cigarette and lit it as we filed into the kitchen. "Over there," she told me, indicating a chrome chair angled out from the table. The little orange kitchen smelled like baby. I came across one, no bigger than a football, in a car seat on the table.

Cigarette on her lip, Mrs. Feiner put on a pair of half-glasses and rolled my pant leg up to the knee.

"It's just a little birdshot," Ronnie told her.

"Hold still," she said to me. She set her cigarette in an ashtray behind the baby. She kept looking over her glasses at me, and I finally told her my name.

"I know who you are. You moved into that house of Grady Blackwell's with your mother."

I nodded.

"What about your dad?" she said.

"They got divorced last year. He stayed in Danbury."

She touched a pellet crater on my shin, her fingers round, the nails short and unpainted. I thought of that strong ring-less hand on the door pull as I climbed the rubber-coated steps. Mrs. Feiner would hit the north lot speed bumps so fast you floated right into the aisle.

"I bet Grady isn't renting it out cheap," she said in a tone that seemed to accuse me of something.

"My mom sells real estate."

"Oh. Well. Fancy." She looked over at Maura, who was rubbing the baby's gums with her finger. "Why don't you do this? I need to look at that window."

Maura picked up the baby in her car seat and set her on the counter next to Ronnie. "Just keep an eye on her, okay?"

"Why can't you?" Ronnie said

"I need to get Band-Aids. She's not going to do anything. Just don't let her fall off."

"I better wash my hands," he said, but then just stared at the baby.

"I'll watch the big scary baby," Mrs Feiner said. She handed Ronnie two pieces of windowsill. "You figure out how these go."

"What are you going to pay me?"

"What are you worth?"

"A six of Moosehead," he said, and I looked at him a little stunned. He wasn't ever this brave at school.

"Is that a fact?" Mrs. Feiner said.

"Or ice beer. Ice is higher alcohol." Ronnie started fitting in the pieces of sill. "I need some woodscrews."

Mrs. Feiner scooted the baby back on the counter and went out the side door into the garage. Ronnie held the wood in place as if waiting for glue to dry. I had two drags from Mrs. Feiner's cigarette and set it back.

"You want to fuck her," Ronnie said.

"You do."

We chuckled with straight faces that denied and admitted it. As an unspoken rule we only confessed to lusting after two or three untouchable girls at school, stuck-up, painted-on-Jordache girls who dated guys that played in metal bands. The running fallacy was that we were without girlfriends only because our standards were so high.

I would have been all for losing my cherry with Mrs. Feiner, except she had a boyfriend named Vernon, whose Monte Carlo was often parked in the driveway next to her car. Vernon cut grass in a few of the big graveyards around town and on weekends sold nun chucks and hunting knives at the flea market behind Chase Middle School. Kids on the bus said he also sold pills that had names like candy: thrusters and black beauties, rainbow rolls and marshmallow reds.

Maura came back with a shoebox full of first aid. She pulled out a chair for herself, lay my leg across her knee, and began rubbing peroxide-soaked cotton up and down my shin.

"What hurts?" she said, and I showed her. Her wavy red hair was drying in an alligator clip, and under a freckled forehead her eyes were medium blue. Maybe in another school she could have been untouchable. I didn't know what governed these things. I did know that for a while she dated Freddy Maxwell, who was probably the most popular guy at school. He always carried two packs of Newports, and if you bummed a smoke he'd give you one for later. When Tammy Cherubini said he knocked her up and he denied it, we naturally believed him. When it happened again with Maura Feiner we took his side again, though our hearts weren't in it this time.

Mrs. Feiner came back with a canning jar full of screws she handed to Ronnie. He took one out and dropped it back. "These are sheet-metal screws."

"It's what I have." She watched him for a moment. "Is Mary really letting you drink beer?"

"Since I was like ten."

"Build me a new air conditioner stand, and you can have a six-pack. Budweiser or Budweiser. Your choice."

I wanted to say something to Maura, the time had come and gone a few times already, and now I said, "What do you charge?"

Her eyes rolled away and her lips flattened. "For what?"

"For being a nurse." Suddenly my heart was rattling like a Superball in a jar. "How about pizza at Cha-Chi's?"

She continued wiping my shin until the cotton balls came away clean, too shy to answer, and that was all right with me. She asked how school was, and I told her, idiotically, that it was out for the summer. She looked at me with a tightness around her eyes that seemed to foretell our first argument as a couple. "I mean last year."

"You didn't miss anything."

"I might come back if my grandmother can baby-sit. They'd make me be a sophomore again."

"You'd be with us," I said.

"Yeah," she said, wiping a fleck of my blood from her thumbnail. "With you guys."

"Don't split the trim," Mrs. Feiner said to Ronnie. "That one's too close to the edge."

"I know what I'm doing," Ronnie said. "I learned this back in Nam." It was a line from a Chuck Norris movie we'd exit-entered at the Twelve-plex.

"Nam, my ass," Mrs. Feiner said. "Just don't split that wood, Nam."

Maura touched the first pellet with the tweezers, and a wave of cold spit flooded my mouth. I pulled my leg back and laughed convulsively, the way you do over dark water just before you jump. "You okay?" she said, and I understood that I would stay after her mother had gone to work. Maura would show me her records, and I'd pick Rush's *Caress of Steel*, third track, "Lakeside Park." Later, in her bedroom, when she told me I did it better than Freddy Maxwell, I'd say, "You're not so bad yourself."

The baby cooed. She wore a little blue Smurfette shirt, and her hair was just wet sparrow feathers on a pink scalp with veins showing through. I looked back at Maura just as she squeezed the fleshy side of my shin, where a gleaming black pellet lifted out like a sliver.

"Why did he shoot you?"

"He snuck up on me," Ronnie said.

"Quit lying," I said.

"He thinks he's Ram-blo."

"Bullshit, Ronnie."

"I told him not to sneak around when you got guns," he said. He could zip himself up so that nothing you said got through. If there was an eyewitness, it wouldn't have mattered. I tried to grin but suddenly I felt close to tears. "He just did," I said to Maura. "He's retarded."

"Hey," Mrs. Feiner said. "You don't need to be calling anybody names." In her glare I saw disgust. But she had no right to judge me. I called him retarded fifty times a day, and he called me retarded, and Mrs. Feiner didn't know how many times I'd let him cheat off me, or how I'd sit at his table in the caf when nobody else would.

An engine grumbled outside, and I heard gravel scatter. Mrs. Feiner watched out the window. "Well, this figures."

"Just lock the door," Maura said.

"I guess his tramp girlfriend finally came to her senses."

"I'm serious, Ma. Don't let him in."

Vernon revved the engine once, the glass-pack mufflers rattling like a pair of Uzis, and shut it off. The thought of him finding a locked door inspired a chain of violent images, and involuntarily I began to stand. My pant leg was still rolled up and Maura, with a Band-Aid half unpeeled, caught me by the knee. "Where are you going?"

I smiled miserably and settled back just as Vernon came in with his hands full of beer and Mountain Dew. He wore jeans with webbed holes in both knees and an Iron Maiden shirt that said, "Can I Play with Madness?"

"You've got some nerve," Mrs. Feiner said.

Vernon glanced at her but kept moving to the refrigerator, where he skillfully opened the door with his elbow. He set the beer and soda inside and opened himself a bottle. He was closer to Ronnie's age than Mrs. Feiner's and had straight black hair to his shoulders. The veins of his neck stood out as though he'd been bench-pressing, and he had gnarled, skinned-up hands.

"Yo. Kid from next door," he said to Ronnie, who chewed a thumbnail and looked at the ground, suddenly the tense, brooding kid he was in the halls of Woodrow Wilson High. Vernon looked at me. "Yo. Other kid. What's shaking?"

"Nothing, man," I said. I was overeager and sounded like a fool.

"It's Ronnie and Dale," Maura said.

Mrs. Feiner came to the table, snubbed out what was left of her cigarette, and picked up the pack of Vantages. "That one shot this one," she said.

"Well, goddamn," Vernon said, and looked at Ronnie. "What'd he do to you?"

Ronnie dropped his screwdriver on the linoleum and picked it up. Vernon watched him a moment, then turned to me. "What'd you, steal his woman?"

"I didn't do anything," I said.

"Who taught you how to install an air conditioner?" Mrs. Feiner said.

"Yeah, I saw. The braces were rotten." Vernon looked at the job Ronnie was doing on the window and sipped his beer.

"Why aren't you out with the skank?" Mrs. Feiner said, collecting the used cotton balls, a fresh cigarette in her lips. The smoke as she looked over it at Vernon gave her an expression of bitterness and doubt. "That Lori Valentino," she said.

"I know who you mean."

"Am I supposed to be jealous? Because I hate to pop your ego."

"You called me, Helen."

"*Ma!*" Maura said.

"Shut up," Mrs. Feiner said. She dropped the cotton balls in the trash. "You better get yourself tested, is all I know."

"What kind of test, driver's ed.?" Vernon said. "Should I take the bus driver test?"

"AIDS would be a place to start."

He folded his arms and grinned. "You found out I'm a fag. Oh, heck."

"Anybody can get it. Watch the news." She leveled her eyes on him. "God, you're stupid."

Vernon leaned back against the counter and looked at Ronnie and me. "So, what's this all about," he said. "You ride the school bus? Helen Feiner's magic school bus?"

"Oh, you go to hell," Mrs. Feiner said and set down her cigarette.

"I used to ride the bus," Vernon said. "And she used to ride me on the bus. Ask her to show you the famous cigarette burn—"

Mrs. Feiner rose up and swung at Vernon, but he caught her wrist, and she swung the other hand and hit him in the ear. He caught that wrist. "The fuck is wrong with you?"

She struggled to free her hands but couldn't. She slumped in his hold, and after a second he let go of one hand, cocked back and slapped her across the face. "Don't pull that shit with me," he said.

Maura threw my leg off and ran to the baby. Mrs. Feiner wrenched her left arm away and stepped back. "Get out," she said. "I'm calling the cops."

Vernon shook his head. "Hysterical Helen," he said. He looked at the floor and then, surprisingly, at me. "Easy kid," he said, and then he turned to Maura. "Your friend doesn't know which way to run."

Maura ignored him, and Vernon leaned back into the counter. "Kid," he said to Ronnie, who had started turning a screw into the sill. "Kid. Jesus Christ." Vernon reached over and knocked the screwdriver from his hand into the sink. "Just be cool," he said to Ronnie. "Just stand there and be cool." He took a drink of his beer.

"Get off my property," Mrs. Feiner said to Vernon. "Fuck you."

Vernon slammed the bottle on the counter, and foam erupted out of the neck.

"You're pathetic," Mrs. Feiner said.

Vernon stared at her. "Do not call me," he said. "Do not come by my work."

"Uh-oh, the big threats. Just do the world a favor and get lost."

Vernon opened the refrigerator, picked up the beer and left the soda. "You ought to get out of this house," he said to Maura. "She'll make you batshit crazy."

Maura looked at him and then at her mother. "Tell him to go," she said.

"What do you think I've been doing?" Mrs. Feiner said.

Vernon closed the refrigerator so hard bottles fell inside, and he walked out. He started the Monte Carlo and raced the engine. There was a small turnaround at the end of the driveway, and he hit it fast and loud. Gravel shot at the house. The old single pane of upper window sash exploded, raining glass into the sink, and Maura threw herself over the baby.

Mrs. Feiner went to the back door, but Maura screamed at her, and then Ronnie lurched across and grabbed Mrs. Feiner by the shoulders. She was already stopped, but he pulled her back in, as he might if there was a tornado funneling around out there. "All right," she said. "Let go of me. I'm not going." Outside the Monte Carlo ran a long burn out in the street.

I stood up and slid the chair back under the table. When I finished rolling down my pant cuff Maura was watching me, her eyes glazed and sad, almost sleepy. In them I saw her already accepting that we wouldn't go out for pizza. That I'd made the offer without understanding anything about her life. After a moment she ripped off a paper towel and wiped up the suds around Vernon's bottle. "You're going to be late for work, Ma," she said.

Mrs. Feiner moved out of the way so I could pass. At the door I looked back at Ronnie. "You coming?" I said.

Ronnie watched me a few seconds then shook his head and fished the screwdriver out from the soaking dishes. I opened the back door.

"Hey Dale," he said, and I turned in the threshold. "When I go get my shotgun, it still better be there." He looked ready to fight all of a sudden, but not like our usual fights, the kind you get over. Mrs. Feiner had her purse opened and was putting on lipstick. Maura poured out the rest of Vernon's beer, and Ronnie began to work another screw into the sill.

Storm Damage

THE WEATHER MAN SAID MIDNIGHT, BUT BY 2 A.M. IT STILL HASN'T come. The sound of surging wind brings Tiffany the last memories of her father. They were driving in his old Bonneville. The storm—was it Gloria? She remembers a shopping cart tumbling through an intersection. He parked in front of Uptown Liquors. Her door didn't work, so he grabbed her under the arm and ran up the sidewalk only to find the store closed, a taped sign that she was just old enough to read: Hurricane. Her father pounded the door and yelled in the wind. Then the rain started and instantly they were soaked. He ran her back to the car to find that he had locked the keys inside. Setting her down he found a piece of brick and smashed in the driver's window. He put her in the back seat and wrapped her with a quilt that smelled of gasoline. Rain pelting the side of his face, he drove around rolling trash cans saying over and over that he was sorry. He was so sorry.

She's long since forgotten being afraid that day. What she remembers is that for a week or so afterward he stayed home at night with her and her mother and only drank beer. Tiffany thought they could all be a family like one of the families on TV. That's what she feels now, listening to storm, that same anticipation of change.

Lamplight flickers, and the deadbolt clacks like a shot. Danny falls into the room and heaves the door closed with his shoulder. The rain-smelling gust he lets in sends mail across the dinette table. "Tiff, you're up, good," he says in a breathless rush. He tosses his leather dart case onto the futon, where he's been sleeping for more than a week, and starts pacing to the kitchenette and back. His hair is all over the place, thick black Tom Cruise hair, the first thing she ever loved about him.

Not quite ready to find out what's wrong, Tiffany looks at the woman modeling Tanzanite rings on the muted TV. "Did the rain start?" she says.

"They said category three? Bullshit. It's going to be a four. You can tell a four." He stops under the ceiling fixture, cranes back with his hands behind his head and staggers. It takes a lot to get him drunk, and she wonders how much he spent at the Overtime. She tells him she's going to bed.

"Tiff, I got mugged," he says. When she looks at him again she sees not the Danny of now, the Danny she's leaving, but the boy his mother talks about, who was picked on at school. His shoulders slump, his eyes blinking with a sudden shine. "Just like twenty minutes ago," he says, "right outside the bar."

The door—he didn't turn the bolt again, and she stares at it unable to move, as if what he's said has followed him home. "Danny. My God."

"I'm getting in the Camino and this guy comes up. It's windy, so I'm thinking he's going to bum a ride. Tiff, he points a Glock up in my face. A freaking Glock." Danny closes his eyes for a moment and touches his temples. "Your mind does these things. Instead of pissing my pants, I'm wondering where this punk Guinea gets a nine hundred dollar gun. I only got like eighteen bucks, and he's pissed but he takes off. Then I go back in and tell Frank, and he runs out looking for the guy, waving *his* piece around. I mean, everybody has a piece. What happened to this fucking town?"

Tiffany fights the impulse to hug him. For a moment she thought he was making it up so she would stay with him out of pity, but now that Frank's been mentioned it's verifiable, and she feels guilty. She does hug him, asks if he's hurt, he's not, and after enough time she pulls back. He holds on to her hand, and there is a long second when she wishes she still loved him.

She pulls her hand away. Danny goes into the kitchenette and takes down a coffee mug and the Absolut from the freezer.

"You've got work tomorrow," she says and yawns, suddenly

ready for sleep. She can postpone knowing if they got his wallet—his Sears card and license.

He pours a shot and drinks it without a sound.

"Stay up if you want," she says, and this time she makes it all the way into the bedroom.

The crash she can feel under her feet. When she comes out to the living room again the front door is wide open, the knob punched through the sheet rock. Like a sidewalk witness to a car wreck she squints into salty electric wind.

Danny appears outside in the stairwell light holding two Beefeaters boxes she'd seen in the dumpster. "Let's do it right now," he says. "Let's pack you up. Fuck it." He heaves the boxes in and slams the door.

"You just ruined the wall," she says. "Good luck getting your deposit back."

At the bookshelf he pulls down her books—on photography, on being your own boss, on European castles—in twos and threes. "You want to hear something hilarious?" he says. "When I almost got shot tonight, I wasn't even scared. I was thinking about you. I was worried how you'd get by."

He picks up the framed picture of Tiffany and her daughter Marcy at Chuck E. Cheese's. She rushes him. "Not in there with the books. What's wrong with you?" Whose fault it is isn't clear, but suddenly the frame falls and its glass shatters on the hardwood floor. "You asshole," she says, and she pounds him with the bottom of her hand.

It happens too fast to see, more of a sound than a feeling, a cymbal crash. Then tingling, heat. She raises her hand again, but suddenly her legs give out and she's on the ground. Danny's hand is still flexing. "Get off me," he shouts, his voice breaking in a sorry plea of self-defense.

The other time she remembers going to bed with a chair propped against the door was when Bert, her mother's third husband, smashed all the potted plants with a framing hammer. Sometime after three she falls into a deep, healing sleep. The sound that wakes her might be music, some distorted metal song behind the walls. It turns into engines revving, then low-flying airplanes. "Stop it," she calls. Her mind lunges back for the sleep she sorely needs. Why is he doing this? It's too late to go out there. By now everything will be broken up on the floor. The thrashing builds and wanes, and her body, like one continuous muscle, flexes to the pulse. She balls up on her side. "Stop it, Danny," she calls again and tries to deafen herself with pillows.

When she wakes a second time, the closed blinds are bright as a movie screen. She touches and then opens her throbbing left eye with her fingers. The clock is out. "Shit." Her shift supervisor has warned her twice about being late. She digs her cell phone out of her purse and has to close her bad eye to read the time. Eleven-oh-five. She calls work but no answer, not the Consolidated Container switchboard operator, not even the machine.

To see in the bathroom she has to open the blinds, and the daylight is excruciating, puddles on the sidewalks gleaming like chrome. No trees grow in the small West Arms courtyard, but the lawn and the sand under the swing set are blanketed in green leaves. A tricycle is wedged behind the monkey bar ladder, and a hoodless charcoal grill on its side has turned a puddle black.

In the bathroom she takes a deep breath, then looks at herself in the mirror.

Storming out of the bedroom she kicks over a box fan. "Look what you did to me," she yells, but the futon is empty. Her books are back on the shelf, as is the picture with its frame glass missing. She has no idea what this means.

From the freezer she takes a bag of peas only half thawed and holds them to her eye, scrolling through saved numbers on her cell phone. When Leslie answers, Tiffany can barely hear her. "Where are you?" Tiffany says. "It's loud."

"The Mermaid. You guys need to get down here."

"I'm not going anywhere with Danny."

"Hang on, I can't hear you. Anyway, the power's out. Sarge is giving away all the keg beer before it goes warm." The sound of a door, and the background noise is gone. "Okay," she says, echoey now. "God, it's like pitch black in here."

"Do you think McCree would let me borrow his truck?" Tiffany says.

"Wait, is it official?"

Saying she's moving isn't that hard. Saying she's going to live at her mother's and take care of Marcy again. But then come the words she's never had to say before. "He hit me." The sudden shaking drains her. She covers her mouth.

"Oh, honey," Leslie says. "Oh no. Talk to me, girl."

In the parking lot she's scraping tacky mounds of twigs and pine needles off the wiper blades of her Civic when a loud metal grating distracts her thoughts for the first time that morning. She takes her sunglasses off the dashboard and follows the sound up Lafayette to the intersection, where men in Discount World aprons scoop plate glass window off the sidewalk with snow shovels.

The day is nothing she could have imagined. The big sycamore that chainsaw crews massacre every few years has gone over and, as though in a final defiance, torn from the sky all power lines on both sides of the street. Under its ripped trunk, the bright blue legs of a postal box stick out like those of a flattened cartoon character. The sun is on her face, and for a wild instant she starts to laugh. It's just everything, the strange lightness of the air in August, the rich blue of the sky, as though a film has been peeled away.

The storm has surpassed all predictions, and she digs the slim Canon digital out of her purse. She snaps a picture of the shoveling men. The view-finder is clear enough without having to remove her sunglasses and possibly draw reactions—especially from the tattooed one with the low ghetto pants, who might approach her and, in some stupid show of chivalry, demand to know who gave her the eye.

Two miles and forty-one pictures later, she has some gems. Shots that might be sellable to a magazine or newspaper: a single-section traffic light wrapped around a utility pole like a tetherball; a pair of sidewalk maples, one in full leaf and the other bare as winter; a flock of confused mallards in a lake of gutter runoff.

She's a little surprised by the disappointment she feels when the downtown buildings look relatively normal. Though the sidewalks, streets, and even brick walls are blotched with wet newspapers, there's no real damage. Slanting duct tape X's dress the closed shop windows. McCree's old Silverado pickup is parked along with other cars she recognizes in front of the Mermaid. The truck bed is plastered with wet leaves, and she opens the tailgate, hops up and kicks what she can out onto the street.

The heavy medieval-looking front door of the bar is locked. After she knocks, a gap is pulled in the blinds and the bolt is thrown. The woman who opens ushers her in quickly. With a conspirator's enthusiasm she explains that it's illegal to operate a pub without electricity, and she bolts the door again.

Tiffany hasn't been in The Mermaid since the beer was green for St. Patrick's Day. Now, a few steps into the dark room, she takes off the glasses and quivering points of light become candles. People stop talking and turn and squint until she is recognized.

Leslie and McCree are on their regular stools in front of the Pabst beer pull. As Tiffany approaches, Leslie spots her in the wall mirror behind the register, stands and embraces her in a deep, urgent hug that makes Tiffany feel a vague pang of guilt. How many times she's been annoyed early in the night by Leslie's vacant cheeriness, how many times in conversation she's just stopped listening. And now coming by only because McCree, Leslie's boyfriend, owns a truck. "Thanks, Lee," Tiffany says. Leslie tightens the hug and says softly, close to her ear, "Danny just lost the best thing that ever happened to him."

"You hang on a little bit, you'll have two helpers," McCree says and looks at his watch. "We're just waiting on Baxter. He's coming by with some property of mine."

Leslie asks a couple to move down. As she takes the warm stool, Tiffany doesn't look around because she doesn't want to be seen. Candles throw shaking bottles on the walls. The swelling blocks peripheral vision in her left eye, and the smoky dark and standing people make her feel vulnerable. Leslie takes a cup from a stack and fills it with foamy tap beer.

"Did I ever tell you about Doug?" Leslie says. "Doug was a long time ago. He was the nicest guy in the world except that rum and Coke turned him into Mike Tyson."

The beer is already sweet. It tastes like the first beer you ever tried, a forgotten cup at a cookout or wedding reception. A drowsy tightening at the base of her scalp tells her she hasn't eaten all day. It spreads through her spine, and she softens. When she's down to foam Sarge comes by and fills her a new cup. She watches his head of wavy white hair until he knocks back the tap handle. "The fire marshal walks in, I'm sunk," he says, grinning even though he can't quite keep the gloom out of his voice. Tiffany and Leslie are two of a group of women he refers to as his "kids" and "cutie pies." But his set-back eyes sag on her now as though the life has gone out behind them. "I'm okay," she says.

"You want me to, I'll speak to him," Sarge says. "Be glad to."

Tiffany smiles uncomfortably. Leslie turns from a conversation, takes hold of her forearm, and pats it. "Poor baby," she says. "You just stay right here next to me." Leslie has deep dimples and glowing teeth when she smiles. She's always been too pretty for McCree. His first name is Sherman, but everyone calls him McCree. It even says "McCree" on the coveralls he wears to work. Today his stringy hair is back in a ponytail, and he wears a T-shirt that says, *Treat me good, I'll treat you better. Treat me bad, I'll treat you worse.*

"Tell her what Junior did," Leslies says to him. "She could use a laugh." Then Leslie turns and pats Tiffany's arm. "This'll cheer you up."

Leaning back on the bar McCree shakes a couple of pretzels

in his fist. "I don't think you know Junior Budo, my downstairs neighbor," he says. "Big Albanian, one earlobe missing. Anyway, Junior drives this decked-out F250 diesel I guess he still owes a shitload on. So he knocks on my door this morning to see if I mind he cuts down that sweet gum in front of the house. What do I care? All it does is piss sap all over everywhere. So he goes out with a chainsaw and drops the fucker right on top of his pickup. You know, for the insurance."

Tiffany nods but feels too exhausted suddenly to laugh. Leslie watches her, blinking, and her eyes glaze over before she turns back to McCree. For the first time Tiffany is envious of their relationship, listless and mismatched as it is. They outlasted her and Danny by a long shot.

"They'll know," Leslie says to McCree. "They'll send investigators."

McCree shrugs. "It fell down. Somebody cut it up."

"He thinks he's smart and the rest of the world is stupid," Leslie says.

"They maybe won't believe it," McCree says. "All I know is, it took balls."

Tiffany takes off her jean jacket and hangs it on the back of the stool. "Is anybody else suffocating in here?" she says. In the mirror she catches Leslie staring, but when she turns Leslie acts like she's only watching the pool game behind them. It's irritating. What's kept Tiffany from calling Leslie wasn't a fight so much as a realization. It happened at a club in Naugatuck. This same kind of thing as now, Leslie watching her furtively, then looking away. Tiffany, just back from dancing with Danny, was a little light-headed. "What?" she said to Leslie.

"These are the good old days, aren't they? All of us here together. I want it to be exactly like this in twenty years." Leslie lifted her glass, and to avoid making a scene Tiffany brought hers up in a toast with her and Danny and McCree. But nothing in the world was more depressing than a woman in her forties partying like she was in her twenties.

There are women like that all around them now in the Mermaid. Women and men, some in their fifties and sixties, smoking, coughing, mixing tomato juice into their Pabst.

"It's so beautiful outside," Tiffany says.

Leslie looks at her. "Are you crazy? It's mayhem out there. And meanwhile I've got a freezer full of melting food I just bought."

"I can't believe we're sitting around getting drunk on flat beer. What is wrong with everybody?" She turns and sees that McCree is watching her. She didn't say it for him to hear, but as though in answer he sucks his beer half-way down. She looks back at Leslie. "Bye. I'm going."

"Look, Tiff," Leslie says. "I know you had a really shitty night, okay? But these people in here happen to be our friends."

The air outside is thick again. Sweat trickles under her blouse, and she can smell the septic plant on Route 8. On the residential end of Meriden Avenue, wood chippers shoot coarse salads of bark and leaf into plywood boxes. High in a bucket lift a Con-Edison worker pokes his gloved hand into a transformer. Except for the white faces of sawed-off tree limbs, she can fully imagine the streets back to normal. She remembers first stepping out into the day, the sun exploding like a flashbulb, the air moving in from the Atlantic and smelling of possibility and change.

Tiffany uses her key and steps into the dim living room of a small chalk-sided Tudor set back from the sidewalk by two rectangles of thatchy lawn. The blinds are closed, as always, against the street. "It's me," she calls, and from the back of the house her mother answers, "In the kitchen." One of Marcy's plastic cereal bowls sits on the coffee table, two bloated nuggets floating in orange milk. Behind the bowl a coiled Tigger blanket lies in a crescent the size of a six-year-old's rear end, as if little Marcy finished her Lucky Charms and disintegrated.

Tiffany's mother, Elaine, is seated at the kitchen table, dressed in a Block Island sweatshirt and old Lee jeans, with a true crime paperback, a glass of something pink and her cigarettes. On the walls hang a picture of some saint, with pussy willows tucked behind the frame, and the poem "Footprints" shellacked on a plank. The latest addition to the décor is a bumper sticker: *God said it, I believe it, that settles it.* Tiffany touches its edge just to make sure it's only magnetized to the refrigerator and not actually stuck there.

"I don't know which was worse," Elaine says. "The storm racket or Marcy sleeping next to me. Twice I woke up with her foot in my boob."

Tiffany drops her purse on the table and sits in the adjacent chair. She picks up Elaine's pack of Vantages. "Where is she?"

"Raking leaves with Phoebe Meyer's grandson. Where're your cigarettes?"

"I quit."

"Since when?"

"The walk over here. I got rid of my pack, but it was sort of a frustration quit."

Elaine takes a cigarette for herself and pushes the heavy glass ashtray between them. "Okay, are you ready for this?" Tiffany says. "It isn't pretty."

Sensation is so out of whack that the air feels like a splash of cold water when she slips off the sunglasses. Elaine watches her for a long moment before reaching over the table and lightly touching the tight skin. "Damn him," she says. "Look that way."

Tiffany stares at the washer and dryer against the far wall. Her mother's white blouse and skirt uniforms from the nursing home are folded in a plastic tub. The kitchen smells like Cuddle fabric softener and the Maxwell House Elaine brews day and night—which would be steaming in the coffee maker now if there was power. Elaine tells her to look in another direction—checking for broken blood vessels, she says—and Tiffany's eyes settle on the pink drink in Elaine's glass. "You're drinking Marcy's Strawberry Quik?"

"To use up the milk. Did you call the cops?"

Tiffany settles back into her seat. She doesn't want to explain, because in the end she'll be defending Danny. Saying it wasn't exactly a premeditated act. Five minutes here, and her perfect blamelessness feels threatened for the first time. She wonders if in fact she and her mother can live together again.

"At least get it on record," Elaine says. "In case he turns into a stalker."

"Did you ever call the cops on Bert?"

Elaine looks down and chips away something dried on the tabletop with her fingernail. Tiffany notices the title of the book in front of her: *September Slaughter.*

"Because it's a little hypocritical," Tiffany says. "Do as you say, not as you do."

"Well, learn from my mistakes," Elaine says. She leans back with her cigarette and sighs. She has a small face with pretty features, eyes the blue of glass, but she looks old. She's too pale with too many wrinkles for a woman in her early fifties. The gray parts of her pulled-back hair are thicker than the brown and won't lie flat, like someone else's hair mixed in, weeds in a lawn.

Tiffany was fifteen when Elaine quit drinking and everything quieted down. They spent more time together afterward, watching Matlock at night over a big steel bowl of popcorn, and Tiffany felt safer. But along with her 7-7s Elaine gave up men and makeup, hair color, and finally friends who weren't church friends.

Elaine sets her cigarette in the ashtray with Tiffany's, and the smoke lifts side by side and blends near the ceiling.

"No alcohol in the house," Elaine says after a while. "I mean that, Tiffany. I don't want to open the refrigerator—"

"I understand, Ma. No alcohol. God and abstinence. I got it."

"And we go to bed early."

"I know you do. I'm not going to disturb your immaculate sanctuary. I just need someplace to live for a little while." The tears are coming up in her throat, but she swallows and sits straighter in the seat. "I just want to raise my daughter. Is that so awful? I want to be her mother again."

"I want that, too," Elaine says. "That's all I've ever wanted."

When the screen door slaps behind them Tiffany snubs out her cigarette. She turns and Marcy appears—her sandy hair wind-blown, the gorgeous hazel eyes of her father shimmering—in the kitchen archway. "It's Marcy Moo-Moo," Tiffany says.

"Mommy, guess what," Marcy says, crossing the linoleum in her Littlest Pet Shop sneakers. "The power broke and the TV doesn't even *work*." She stops five feet shy of Tiffany and her mouth hangs open. "What happened?" she says, inching closer. "Gross."

"A door knob got me."

"They only come up to here, Mom," Marcy says and shows her how high. "You got punched."

Tiffany keeps up her smile, though her daughter's open stare makes her life feel like an episode of *Jerry Springer*. "You know what I need?" Tiffany says. "A great big giant hug. The biggest hug that ever happened. Know where I can get one?" But Marcy is already walking away, past the refrigerator, to stand on a plastic step and pick up the wall phone. "Who are you calling?" Tiffany says.

Marcy dials and puts the phone to her ear. "Danny. I'm gonna tell him come over here so I can give *him* a punch."

The spare bedroom has a futon, a dresser with stickers all over it, a shallow closet with bi-fold doors. Tiffany sits on the floor while Marcy pulls coloring books down from a shelf and stacks them in a toy box under the window. At least half of them are Bible books—*A Journey with Jesus. Moses and the Commandments.* Tiffany opens

Noah Fills the Ark. Inside the pictures are carefully crayoned inside the lines. Even the colors are right—orange tigers, yellow giraffes. "So where are the dinosaurs?" Tiffany says.

"He couldn't fit them," Marcy says immediately, as though she was ready for the question. "That's how come there aren't any left."

Tiffany sets the book down and brushes the thick mane of a toy pony. "Do you keep turning on light switches? I mean even when you know the power's out?"

Marcy shrugs. "It's not dark out yet. This is my braids and ponytails book, Ma, if you want to borrow it."

Tiffany watches Marcy take down stuffed animals and organize them by size on the floor. "Let's see," Marcy says. "You over here." Tiffany thinks of her daughter's hands when they had dimples instead of knuckles, when surprises made her laugh—a giant sheep dog somebody brought over, a burst pipe in the bathroom.

"Moo," Tiffany says. "Do you remember before you lived with Grandma?"

"Kind of," Marcy says, dusting an empty shelf with a sock.

"That apartment over the bakery? That great bread smell we used to wake up to?"

"The Christmas tree caught on fire," Marcy says.

"That was our first Christmas there. And your dad put it out with my Diet Coke, remember? We ended up leaving it on the fire escape because it stunk."

"Why didn't he just use water? Didn't we even have a sink?"

"Of course we did. It was a nice apartment."

Marcy shrugs and brushes her hands together after dusting. "There," she says.

"My life isn't completely terrible, you know. There were happy times."

Now she's stacking Beanie Babies in a shoe-box. "Ma, if you need any of these for decorations, they'll be in here."

"You know that, right?" Tiffany says. "We had fun. You used to laugh all the time."

"Tiff," Elaine calls from out in the kitchen.

"Everyone used to say how happy you looked."

"Tiff."

"What, Ma?"

"What is that car of Danny's?"

She looks out into the kitchen. "An El Camino. Why?"

Elaine covers the phone receiver. "For the neighborhood watch. Do you know the license plate?"

Tiffany closes her eyes and tries to breathe. But all at once her lungs stop working and her fingers stab out at the ground like steel blades. In a red surge she grabs the nearest thing—a Beanie Baby, a seagull—and hurls it at the dresser. "Fuck."

Marcy lights out of the room. Panting, Tiffany steps over the shoe-box and goes to the window. She hears Elaine say, "Baby, it's not your fault."

She touches her eye to the cool glass. Across the street some kids are jumping into a pile of raked-up leaves. The leaves are still green with little bits of branch attached. By the curb the father tries to rake, and the kids keep jumping through his piles.

In a while a pair of small hands comes around her waist. "I'm not mad at you," Tiffany says, realizing she had no idea what she'd do if Marcy hadn't come back. She looks down at her daughter's beautiful blonde head. Marcy is watching out the window.

"Those kids throw crabapples at cars sometimes," she says.

Stroking her hair, Tiffany looks quietly out the window, and together they watch the neighborhood kids play in the heavy summer leaves.

Rip Off

AFTER HIGH SCHOOL I TURNED WRENCHES IN A SOUTH WATERBURY basement we called The Dungeon. It was two small bays with fieldstone walls, a dirt floor that swallowed sockets and in the fall sprouted little black mushrooms. Sometimes you didn't know if it was day or night outside. But it was the kind of work I loved, general auto repair that called for aptitude and dexterity and zero people skills. Ray Dugan didn't send me to customer service seminars or make me wear a uniform. He was an old school mechanic who could tear an engine right down to the crank—even the carburetor in a hundred pieces—store it in five-gallon buckets while the owner paid on installments, then have it back together and idling like glass in an afternoon.

A few nights a week we'd pick away at one of these long-term installment jobs over a case of Schafer and New England Rock 101on the boom box. I'd get home late and Justine would expect some kind of apology. We had fights. Our bedroom was two doors down from her parents in a new subdivision that felt much further than it was from The Dungeon, with its aroma of gasoline and cigarette butts and flat beer in a hundred fingerprinted cans.

Ray and I were overhauling the 302 engine in an old Crown Vic on the night there was trouble. I was telling him how he could make some easy money. At that time the only thing keeping Ray afloat was that he took cash payments from drug dealers when the mayor's strategic plan encouraged businesses to accept checks and credit only.

My idea was to buy one of the old interface oscilloscopes that Precision Tune upstairs was selling off. "All we need is one," I said to Ray. "We can do computer work cheap and put them out of business with their own equipment."

Up to his elbows in cast iron and grease, Ray torqued a head bolt. "In theory, okay. But how much would they want to soak me, Davey?"

"He's asking two, but I could talk him down to seventeen or eighteen a scope." I tried to sound more certain than I was. Last week I was picking out a grinder off the roach coach when Clifton, the shop manager upstairs, came out and handed me a card. He was looking for a new brake man, part time to start. "Ray's a good guy," he said. "I like Ray. But kid, you have to realize you're on a sinking ship down there."

Screw that asshole. If he was firm on two, I'd chip in the extra myself.

Ray stretched his neck side to side, his big cinder block of a head still in a military cut. His teeth were bad, his coughs were wet, and the lines on his face looked deep enough to hold coins. "Yeah," he said. "Gone I guess are the days when you got by with a wrench and a decent ear." He walked to the potbelly stove and broke up a pallet board. The coals made that dry pop like strings of ladyfingers. It was late December, almost Christmas, and out through the scratched bay door window, sleet shot around in the wind. I looked at the wall clock, its hands just visible through rag streaks in the grime.

"You need to go, go on," Ray said.

"I'm good." Justine was home expecting me either to call or show up, but it wasn't late yet. Not that late.

There came a thump on the bay door, and in the little window appeared the bulging black face of Jimmy Southard, whose Chevy big-block engine was waiting on a payment in the next bay.

"Come on around," Ray yelled. "I'm not letting my heat out."

Jimmy came in the side door with a stringy-haired white guy, both of them steaming wet. The door blew back, and the white guy hit it with his weight just as the wind died so that it slammed hard.

"Which one of you is shelling out for a new door?" Ray said to Jimmy.

Jimmy looked at the white guy. "Why you tearing the place down?"

"Talk to the wind," his buddy said.

Jimmy took off a fur-lined hat, and his big shaved head glistened under the chain-hung fluorescents. "Ray, this is Scotty," he said. "Scotty, Ray."

Our hands were always too black to shake, and they just traded nods.

"Black ice all the way up Andover," Jimmy said, rubbing his hands. "I went down twice on that bitch." He had to weigh three hundred pounds, and falling on the ice would be something to see. In most settings Jimmy was a dangerous man, but now he wiped sleet from the sleeve of his long leather coat and grinned sort of boyishly. "Davey, I heard your old lady failed the stick test."

"She's due in March," I said.

He took out a box of White Owls he used for blunts and handed me one still in plastic. "Good on you, dog," he said.

Scotty wandered over to the woodstove. The radio was playing classic rock on a workbench, and Scotty watched it as though it were a TV as he rubbed his bony hands.

"You come by to pay for that motor?" Ray said to Jimmy. He didn't like visitors at night, not in this neighborhood. We were two blocks from the Rocky Hill projects, where Jimmy did his dealing and trouble came cheap.

"How's she looking?" Jimmy said. Though he sounded hopeful, he had eyes in his head and could see that nothing had been done. The engine had a phone book and two crushed Schafer cans sitting on top of it.

"Same way it looked a week ago," Ray said. "Not paid for."

"I got it. We're cool." Jimmy pulled out a bankroll too big for his hand to close around. "How much?"

"Half."

"*Half*? No, man, hold up. I wasn't prepared to hear no motherfucking half."

"I told you to put half down the day you brought it in."

"Raymond," Jimmy said, massaging the back of his head. "I thought you'd do me better than that. You're cutting me where I live."

Ray dropped his wrench on a tool cart. His forearms were covered in grease to the last letters of the *Dead Cong/ Good Cong* tattoo on his big forearm, and the shimmering hair stood out like reeds in a swamp. Silence didn't bother him. He was genuine in that way, and around him I felt safe.

"Four-oh-two," Jimmy said, looking at his engine. "I just located the exact car I want to drop it in. Sixty-six Impala."

Ray picked under his thumbnail with a chisel edge, and I thought, What would that Clifton do right now? I knew damn well what he would do—choke, and stammer for a line from customer service school. But Ray showed no interest in speaking to him again. It was a glorious showdown. I was glad to have stayed late to witness it.

"That's the day I was born twenty-nine years ago," Jimmy said. "Four-oh-two-sixty-six. That's going to be my ride."

"Half or get it out of here," Ray said. "I'm not running a storage unit."

"Ain't that a bitch," Jimmy said. He counted out eight hundreds and looked at the rolling cabinet toolbox for a place to stack it.

"In that middle drawer, there," Ray said, and Jimmy set the money inside and then added another bill.

"Ah, fuck it," he said, counting out more. "There's all of it. There's the whole fifteen." He still had a fat wad left that went back in his deep front pocket.

From the little Frigidaire Ray brought out a beer for himself and one for Jimmy. "There's some hospitality," Jimmy said, and killed it, I swear, in two swallows. He wiped his mouth and looked over at where Scotty was sitting on top of a short stepladder. "Get on over here," he said. Scotty stuffed his hands in his pockets and joined us. "I told him you might be looking to hire at some future date," Jimmy told Ray. "Scotty's new in town. He does..." He looked at Scotty. "You got a tongue, man. What do you do?"

"Change oil. Tune-ups, transmissions, brakes, name it," Scotty said.

"Scotty did a little time for some stupid shit in Pennsylvania," Jimmy said, "so he don't expect no salary situation right away. Maybe you could start him on commission. Like a percentage of what he —"

"I know what it means," Ray said. He looked at Scotty. "You got tools?"

He nodded. "Enough to get going."

"Come by Monday morning. We'll talk."

Scotty rubbed under his chin and looked at Jimmy.

"That's all we get?" Jimmy said, and before Ray could answer he said, "All right, all right. You guys stay warm in here." To me he said, "Tell your lady good luck."

"Will do," I said, and I gloried maybe a little too much in his attention. On impulse I said to Scotty, "Easy on the door."

He turned and cut his eyes at me. "Say what?"

"Scotty, man," Jimmy said, and he dropped a big hand on his shoulder. Ray was already back under the hood at this point, and I was glad. His seeing this would've made me repeat myself and stand by it, and that was the last thing I wanted to do.

When they were gone, Ray said, "That Jimmy's some kind of crap merchant, ain't he?"

"You really want to hire that guy?"

"Straight commish, off the books? I oughta at least consider it." He straightened from the Ford and went over to the toolbox. "If he remembers on Monday—which ten-to-one he won't—I'll put him on that transverse Caddy and see how long he lasts."

Ray took out his wallet, but instead of putting in Jimmy's money he counted out his own bills and laid them on top. "That's seventeen-forty," he said. "See if he takes that for one of them scopes upstairs."

I stared at him as he closed the drawer, my face warming, wanting to say that he wouldn't be sorry, this would change everything, but you didn't talk that way around the shop.

"You want to be the chief negotiator in this thing?" he said. "Just get the one you want, not the one he tries to sell you."

Ray's office was a metal desk, folding chair and two rusting file cabinets pushed back in a corner. I turned up the radio a little— one of the Queensryche songs you heard ten times a day—and sat down to call Justine.

The TV was on in the background when she answered. "I think he's driving a bumper car around in there," she said. We didn't know the sex of the baby, but she said "he" for my sake. In two months the nurse would introduce me to my little girl, and Justine would tell me she was sorry. It bothered me that she would apologize for something like that, and the experience of holding my daughter for the first time was lost to it.

"Are you on your way?" she said. "I made sloppy joes."

"Like another hour, hour and a half." I lowered my voice for the lie I didn't want Ray to hear. "He asked me to stay. It's a two-man job."

She was quiet, and just before I said her name, she said, "One of the strands on the tree is out. I'll let you figure out which bulb it is."

I asked who was home downstairs. It was a pain in the ass living with her parents. Our sex had to be quiet, our fights whispered. Her mother was checking our deposit bags outside for beer cans— like nineteen-year-olds were going to sit around cracking Yoohoos all night.

Everyone was home, and her little sister was up in our room with Justine watching *Murder, She Wrote*. They'd just got done baking cookies.

"You didn't sign the cards again," she said.

"Shit." Christmas was in three days. "Just sign them for me."

"Even your mom's? What about your dad's?"

"What are we even sending him one for?"

"Because it's Christmas, Dave. Because you should try to be forgiving one day of the year."

I felt the familiar throb of pulse in my throat. "Where's his card to me?" There was some noise out in the shop, the door slamming again, and I lowered my voice. "Send it if you want," I said. "Your name only."

After a few moments she said, "That's the Christmas spirit." I heard her little sister ask where the remote was, and Justine said, "Where it always is." Then to me she said, "We made you a cookie shaped like a screwdriver."

"Is it vodka flavored?"

She was quiet again, and I heard her sigh. "I don't feel like bribing you tonight. You'll come home when you come home, I guess." We finished the call, and I hung up with the familiar feeling of not knowing what she wanted from me, or if I was even the one who could provide it.

When I got back to the bays Scotty was there again, standing with his hands in his jacket pockets beside the Crown Vic. I didn't see Jimmy. Ray was shaking his head in a drowsy way. "What's going on?" I said.

Scotty looked at the corner from where I'd come and wiped his nose.

"How in the hell exactly," Ray said to Scotty, "you expect to get hired, you can't follow simple instructions?"

Scotty smirked, and I felt relieved. No way was Ray giving this asshole a job. "What instructions would that be?" Scotty said.

"Does this look like Monday to you?" Ray said.

Scotty shook his head at the ground, and he laughed in a way that told me all that was about to happen. Out of his jacket pocket he brought a small brown pistol. He didn't point it but just held it out a little from his waist like you'd hold hot coffee. "I need that fifteen hundred," he said.

There are moments you surprise yourself, and now, my not screaming or running or crying was one of those moments. I shifted my eyes to concentrate on Ray, who pushed his hands into his front pockets and for a few seconds looked at the floor. Then, very slowly, he looked up at Scotty and said, "You're kidding."

"Get it."

"That cash went in the safe," Ray said. "'Fuck You' is the combination."

"No, fuck *you*, old man," Scotty said, and moved past me over to the toolbox. He opened the middle drawer and stuffed the money in his pants pocket. "This whole town's so fucked up, " he said. "You think I'd work in this shit hole?"

When Scotty turned to me I saw into the gun barrel, a fluted little hole the black of outer space. His long finger, its nail chewed way down, was pushed against the side of the trigger. "Go ahead and piss your pants, bro," he said. "You look like you want to. Should I take it easy on the door?"

But I stayed where I was, and something happened after the first shock wore off. I wasn't afraid. Your mind will do things. When I used to think about Ray being in Vietnam, it made me wonder how I'd hold up in combat. I'd start to breathe heavy—I'd want to lurch at the danger, as if that could cure me of doubt or cowardice. I was surprised now to be calm and thinking. Scotty had said those things to make me feel like a punk, the way my father would talk when he wasn't going to hit me. When he used to hit me he did it without words, with ice in his eyes.

What I thought was this: Shooting somebody was a hundred times the crime robbery was.

"I see you around, you're a dead man," Ray said, not dramatically but as though it were normal talk—pick up your Buick after three—and Scotty swung around with the gun. "Man, if *I* ever see *you* around—"

It came on me like a reflex, my body seeing the opening before my mind caught up, and I launched myself at Scotty, tackling him into a hill of beer cans. The gun never fired and was gone, thrown from his hand, and I pulled back to look at him. "Man, all right," he said, pushing at the floor as cans kicked out under his feet. "Get off."

I pummeled him with both hands, maybe a punch landed for every three or four I threw, but I didn't let up. He kept jouncing, and I could feel how skinny his legs were under mine. There was nothing to him at all. I swung wildly and broke my finger on his forehead—just a sound and a tingle, but enough to say I could still lose this fight. I pushed off him, and from a nearby tool tray I picked up a three-foot socket extension as he kicked at me with his heels. That steel extension was as good as a sword. Across the neck, and his head would've rolled—he realized it at the same moment I did. "*Enough,* man," he said.

Time slowed, and I looked over just as Ray was getting off his knees. He hiked his pants, and I understood as you do in a panic— your perception super-human—that he had been under the car going after the gun, had come up empty, and now he was going around the other side for it. But he looked at me, at the extension gripped in both hands. He neither approved nor disapproved, and I knew that when it was over we would be equals in some way. He'd know what I was made of.

The extension sliced the air as I stepped forward, swinging as to ring the carnival bell, and it caught one of the floor joists overhead. Fire exploded in my broken finger, and the extension bounced away. Almost at the same time something burst through my intestines. Scotty's foot retracted from my nuts like it was spring-driven, and he scrambled away. I fell over, though somehow I was able to chunk a can of brake cleaner in his direction—it missed by a mile. He was out the door before he ever got fully upright.

All this—the tackle, the fight, the escape—happened in less than a minute. Ray was just fishing out the gun with a pry bar. "You all right?" He watched me for a moment before he bent for the gun. When the first full breath hit my lungs I had about three seconds to make it to the bathroom. The plywood door slapped behind me as I lunged over the bowl. My insides jerked and brought up mostly beer. My tonsils burned, and after, as I was sucking at tap water, I heard Ray on the phone. In the little cracked mirror over the sink I looked like a corpse with moving eyes. Even my lips were white.

When I came out Ray was holding the gun. "Three-eighty," he said. "Christ. Look at this pea shooter." He pinched the grip with his thumb and finger and caught the magazine when it fell. A live round waited at the top, angled up like a missile on a tiny launch pad. He pushed it out, and another leapt to replace it.

Ray gave me one of his strong Winstons, and we sat on milk crates by the stove and smoked. You could hear the tips crackle when we inhaled. It was the best cigarette of my life, the one that's made it impossible for me to quit since.

Ray stared off at the front of the shop. Once in a while he shook his head with a foul look. "I tell you what," he said, finally. It was all he said.

I waited on the long sigh you'd think something like this would bring. Finally, I said, "I thought we'd be moving a body." This was off a joke he'd told me about friendship: A friend will help you move, but a true friend will help you move a body. We laughed then, laughed hard, and it seemed like the noblest thing we could do. Ray sat a while panting, recovering from the laugh. Then he said, "Go on home. Get some ice on that finger."

"You going after him?"

Ray looked up at the clock. "Soon as Manny Shorb gets here."

I told him to check Bunker Hill Park, which was where junkies and bums and assholes hung out. He nodded, said he planned to. We started new cigarettes, and the first thing that came to me I asked. I asked what Vietnam was like. I asked if he'd had any close calls.

"Just one," he said. "I had to swim, and I can't swim."

I smoked, staring off, and then thought of something. "You couldn't swim, and you were in the Navy?"

Ray leaned back on his milk crate. When he laughed his eyes in the light were blue and clear, and you could see what he might have looked like as a young man a hundred years ago. He settled forward, hands on his knees, and started to cough.

"What did you do after? Get drunk?"

He shook his head. "I wanted to write this gal a letter, but I didn't have no paper. It would have been nice to have a piece of paper in that fucking war." He laughed again and wiped off a tear. "Jesus Christ, this night." Then he got up and brought over the beers we'd been drinking. He watched me for a few seconds, and I saw the gleam of youth dull from his eyes. He looked up at the clock. "Finish up," he said.

And those two words have stayed with me, how he said them, the command, and the way I felt taken care of afterward. I drank the beer empty and crushed the can and tossed it in the pile. Then I waited for whatever he said next. I was ready for the rest of my life to happen alongside Ray, who was looking out for me now and always would be.

As we were working Go-Jo up and down our arms, the water steaming in the nasty fiberglass sink, Manny, who was Ray's age or older, appeared in the little window. He pounded on the bay door. "I'm in the car," he called.

"You want me to come?" I said, and then like I meant it, "I'll come."

"You go on home," Ray said. He looked at me and sighed the long sigh that meant we'd survived something here, and he clapped a hand on my shoulder. "We'll get him," he said.

Outside the rain had stopped but it was colder, about to snow. My Firebird was parked not far from the side door, and I started the engine and sat there breathing smoke, waiting for the fast idle to kick down. The defroster warmed a pair of clear eggs up the windshield, and by the streetlight I saw Manny parked in his Cutlass. Pretty soon Ray came out and knocked on the driver's-side window, wanting to drive.

Manny got out and held an aluminum baseball bat straight in front of him, as if checking a pool cue. He and Ray grabbed hands, and then Ray looked over at me, for just a second, but enough time that my throat swelled with a feeling like pride.

They wouldn't get Scotty or the money. And Jimmy had four days left of freedom before they'd catch him in the mayor's big sting operation that would cost him eight years of his life up in Osborn. The money and my hopes for an oscilloscope were gone, but it wouldn't really matter. In less than a year, Ray's lung biopsy would come back swimming with cancer, and he'd sell the shop for a song to Clifton, whose offer to hire me was no longer open. But of course I didn't know any of that. This was still in that more or less uncomplicated time when everything seemed to be hanging together. I didn't see the bad road Justine and I were already headed down. I had no idea that being alone was the worst possible thing.

I was satisfied, perhaps for the first time in my life—something was proven that night—and I brought my hand up and waved. As Ray watched me, an easiness came over him, as if it weren't windy and cold, as if he might speak in a low voice that I would be able to hear. But he never opened his mouth. In the end he just jutted his chin once and got in the car.

Between Gravities

ONE NIGHT AT THE RECKLOOSE MY GIRLFRIEND CALLED ME
an emotional retard (the jukebox was changing songs, so everyone
heard), and I told her she was fat and that, after six months, I had
come to realize she would *always* be fat. After that I was single two
years straight. I'd had trouble before holding a steady job, and I'd
scraped with the law under circumstances that resulted in fines
and community service, but nothing can hollow your soul like
spending the night with a radio you're afraid to turn off, imagining
the dee-jay as being exactly too pretty for the man you are. Old
romances that should have amounted to something I'd think
through backwards, from last fights to pre-fucking, like starting a
pencil at the end of the maze and tracing to all the possibilities in
the center.

My confidence was running on fumes when Carol's Citation
rattled into Doc's Motorwerke on four bad plugs and a sticking
float. Carol was thirty-seven and alone except for a son named
Tommy, who was five years old. There was a crazy ex-husband
recently out of the picture, and in the space of an afternoon Carol
and Tommy fled from the people of their life in the hopes of never
laying eyes on him again. All this she told me a few hours into
our first date while Addicted to Sacrifice was between band sets.
I shook my head to say, It disgusts a normal guy like me that this
whacko loser son of a bitch ruined love for you—let me show you
better. But there was also a part of me that understood the man.
Carol was a stunner even at her age, a slim blonde with purple eyes
you wanted to crawl inside, but I imagined her a different kind of
beauty ten years earlier, a woman who could set your heart on fire
if you tried to love her.

On a night in December we were in bed watching the Creature

Double Feature on Carol's small rabbit-eared set. There was a metallic funneling sound behind the walls from air pockets in the radiator piping, whose fluctuating heat had left me under a sheet in my boxers and Carol on the spread in her terrycloth robe. We were holding hands and had been like that for two hours, resting.

A car chase reminded Carol of an accident on Route 8 that morning. She said that one of the men involved got out of his car and started beating the other man with his fists all around the median. "He could've murdered the guy," she was saying. "And I mean over what? The cars were junkers."

I killed my beer and set it back on her bedside table. It was after midnight, and I had a good resilient buzz I figured I'd ride off into Sleepville.

"And the whole time he kept shouting, 'Learn how to drive.' Like it even mattered at that point."

"It helps you win," I said, and she looked at me. "You want to keep up that adrenaline." I air-boxed a couple of tight undercuts.

Carol picked a fleck of lint off her knee and shook it away. "It's because hate isn't natural. You have to psyche yourself up, or get driven to it, I guess. Something a whole lot worse than a fender-bender."

"I've known a few haters," I said.

"I guess it's how I'm wired. I love Tommy without trying, and I love you that way. But hate you have to psyche yourself up for."

Suddenly that old panic started, a light sweat, a tickle in the gut. Get out now, it tried to say. But the feeling passed more quickly than it ever had, and I was exhilarated. "Why don't you say that again?" I said.

"You mean the L-word?" she said and grinned in the lamplight. "It doesn't bite, Jerry. And if I held it in because of how you might take it, I guess that would make me a bullshitter." She placed my hand next to me, clicked off the TV, and got out of bed. At the far end of the room she opened one of the bi-fold closet doors and brought out a golf club. "I'm not sure what other virtues are still intact," she said, "but one thing no one can call me is a bullshitter."

Across from a rubber putting cup she set down a handful of the dimpled white balls. Her first shot nicked the side bank, mostly the fault of a hardwood floor whose boards, worn rough of varnish, pitched in the centers. The ball floundered back out and stopped. "I love you, Jerry," she said. Carol had this way of smiling suddenly that always surprised me. She tilted her head, exposing a soft curve of white neck, and said, "I think it's because you're a mechanic. You see what's happening on the inside. The little triggers that make the big results." Her fingers closed like falling dominoes around the club grip.

"I love you back," I said. "I guess we're even." It wasn't my first time saying it, but my first time meaning it. And it occurred to me that most people I knew around, some even that I felt inferior to, were bitter at heart and lonesome.

The bedroom door rattled suddenly. Its knob was loose in the stile and he couldn't twist it enough to open. When Carol saw me sit forward she held out her hand. "Get in the closet."

"Carol."

"Jerry, please. I can't think."

I pulled on my pants and lumbered across the room, heavy with knowing the night was about to last longer than I'd planned on. In the closet I steadied myself between hanging blouses that smelled like static and vanilla perfume, watching through the middle louvers as she opened the door. Tommy burst across the threshold and latched onto Carol's leg. He coughed and shivered, only wearing sweat pants. "Make it quit!" he said, tears spraying off his lips. "Don't let it. Stay here." In the gap between louvers I could just see his expression, a pleading, panicked look to make your heart kick. I thought of the look on a guy I'd been drinking with a few minutes before he turned himself in to the police. Like even your friends can't help you.

Carol took his face in the crook of her neck and stared

across the room. Her eyes stopped at points along the floor as if measuring distances. There was an ease about her like she'd known these nights before, though I couldn't say since I'd been sleeping at her apartment only once a week, and for less than a month. As I adjusted my footing a plastic hanger scraped my neck. I wiggled my finger between two louvers and scratched the paint just a little. It seemed like enough sound for someone who knew I was in there, but she didn't look in my direction. I pulled my finger back and counted to five. Then I opened the closet door and stepped out.

Carol closed her eyes for a moment after she'd seen me, and when she opened them her look was vague though I didn't think angry, and I said, "It was just a bad dream." Tommy jerked back from his mother and tried to break free, but Carol held him firmly around the waist. "Look, honey," she said. "Who's that? See? It's only Jerry."

"It's only me," I said. His face was sticky with tear tracks that ran down his midget pot-belly all the way to the waistband of his sweat pants. His red hair was pasted across his forehead. "Let *go*," he screamed, writhing against his mother's grip. He slapped the fat bottom of his hand against her side: "I hate you! Let go!"

"Easy, partner," I said, and held his tight little shoulder blade. As though only now waking out of his nightmare, he gazed up at me. "How come you came here, Jerry?" I smelled urine on him and in reflex drew my hand away. Carol frowned, and Tommy lifted his arms around her neck and watched me—pinning me inside a long embarrassing second. "I don't want him, Mommy," he said, softly now. "Let's take me back to bed."

When Carol got back I was under the sheet again. She crossed the room and lifted open the window that faced Manny's Pizza on Lafayette. From the chain-linked front yard white December air curled in, and somewhere nearby a car chirped its tires and tore off.

"It was a nightmare about before, wasn't it?" I said. "About your ex-husband?"

Carol brought a short black tube out of her bureau, the kind used for camera film, and went over to the window with a pack of matches. She sat on the floor and pulled her robe tighter. "I asked you to stay in the closet."

"When do I stop being a stranger around here?" I said. She blinked at me distantly. I thought about going into the living room and turning on the TV. I thought about cracking a few beers. "When does Jerry ever get a break?" I said.

Carol took a marijuana joint out of the tube and lit it, closing her eyes with the first hit, and though a few tokes would have done me no harm she wasn't offering any. She let it out through the window. "His face is so peaceful when he sleeps," she said. "If only the fucking demons would stay away." She hit twice more, then tapped the end of the joint and dropped it into the tube.

When she came back to bed I could see that the thing we'd ended up on different sides of was over for her now. There didn't have to be more unless I was starting. She untied her robe and compressed her shoulders so that it fell all at once to coils around her ankles. "Here I am," she said, her voice soft and willing. I smiled because it was something she'd said before, the night after our first date, when from the bathroom she paused in the doorway, unexpectedly naked as I bobbled off my shoes. She was a small woman, petite, spare and bony in the hips—hard to believe she'd had a baby. There was this dryness to her skin I associated with her age, and her breasts dimpled into all their freckles under a light touch. On the inside of her thigh was an amateur tattoo of a swan, a stringy figure, black-green like an old bruise. There was a good Irish-run parlor downtown where I'd had mine done, and I thought I'd take her there soon for a nice color job, one we'd both pick out.

Carol spun the alarm dial of the clock radio and a split-second of lead guitar blared. She lay beside me and placed my hand near her navel, over stretch marks that felt like tree bark. She turned off the nightstand lamp so that light from a pole outside lipped in over the ceiling and gave us silver outlines.

"It won't get easier later on," I said, wanting that to be the last word of it.

Carol was quiet, though I could feel her nodding slowly, and the thing she was staring at, that I trained my own eyes on, was a funnel of cobweb riding drafts in a ceiling corner. For long seconds it wouldn't connect or let go. Then she rolled over and we had twenty minutes of make-up sex. After, she touched my lips with a finger. "Give us a while," she said. "We're still okay." And I closed my eyes and drowned in sleep that was thick with meaningless dreams I hadn't known in years.

Carol liked to call me at Doc's Motorwerke during her half-hour between work and picking up Tommy from daycare. I planned my lunch break around this time, in the parts room where there was a swivel chair and a desk to put my feet on. Our shop had an arrangement with a half-way house on the north end of Bridgeport, and the mechanics they sent us wore gold studs in their ears and knew more about breaking into cars than fixing them. I pulled them off commission jobs for warranty work, and they gave me the kinds of looks you'd be a fool to turn your back on. So when one of them came in for a computer sensor or spark plugs I'd say something sweet to Carol over the phone. It was cheap, I knew, but it made me feel lucky. She would call from Sikorsky's, where she inventoried gears and fasteners for military helicopters. I knew the factory only as background noise, but as she told me her small plans for the night I imagined massive vats behind her catching bright red fountains of iron.

On the day of the first real snow Carol put together her tree and invited me over. It was a white hemlock imitation with spiraled wire for a trunk, the kind stores buy for their own decoration. The balls were solid blue and solid silver, which didn't make the tree look any friendlier, but the dark paneling in the living room was better for the blinking lights, and I told her it was pretty. I'd brought a quart of eggnog that turned out to be spoiled, so I ran across the street to City Sliquors for a six-pack of beer.

Carol needed to make a few phone calls after dinner, so I went out into the living room with Tommy. Usually he was set for bed by the time I came over, and all I ever saw of him was a tired face stamped by upholstery creases, blinking indifferently at me while his mother carried him off to bed. But he was awake now, and I volunteered a comfortable distance of sofa between us. On TV the dentist elf was setting out for the Island of Misfit Toys. Two cards were butted together over the set, and I noticed that one of them was the same wish of peace and prosperity People's Bank had sent me. On the wall across from us were two framed photographs of white-tail deer, antlered bucks poised in haughty stances over rugged, snow-blanketed country.

"That's what I want," Tommy said as a toy commercial ran. "Except the green kind with the other buttons." After a few seconds he looked at me. A cold tall boy rested between my legs, and I kept bending the tab back and forth. "Okay," I said. "What's that, a squirt pistol?"

Tommy stared at me vacantly until my question lost meaning, and we were involved in the kind of complex quiet where if one of you doesn't smile soon some meanness will probably come of it. A tightrope quiet you call it. So I smiled. Tommy waved me near and I leaned in. "You should have a dog," he said into my ear. And then with his cold hands he pulled my face closer and kissed me in an area under my eye, a small, wet kiss. It was unexpected, and I felt the way you feel when you catch a woman breast feeding, like it's innocent enough but just the same. With his open hand on my forehead he pushed me lightly back.

"What am I going to do with a dog?" I said. Tommy looked at me like I hurt his feelings. "Did you have a dog?" I said.

"Roxy first. We got Ginger after." Tommy stood on the sofa, the back of his hair lifting with static. Then he laughed a mighty shout of a laugh. "Once daddy put Ginger in the bathtub with me. Cause she was mudd-eee. Mudd-eee!"

A door clicked shut down the hall. Tommy was watching me.

"So did your dad keep Ginger?"

Tommy climbed onto the armrest and steadied himself in his alligator slippers. He bounced knees-down off the cushions, and then he got up and did it again, like he'd gotten into rocket fuel. "Ginger drinked anti-freeze," he said, fidgeting now with a throw pillow. He heaved it high over his head and slammed it against his thighs. He did this until he was red in the face, and just before he hurled the pillow at the TV screen he yelled once for each slam, "Ginger—drinked—anti-freeze." And then he plopped back down and sat squirming on his hands, and his program had been running but both of us were staring with surprise and curiosity at the dust-blown place where the Christmas cards had been.

"Do you need your mom?" I said. I wasn't angry and didn't want to come off as if I were. I guessed he'd just had some sort of episode. Tommy hesitated a moment, then shook his head no. He wiped his mouth on his wrist. "Ginger sometimes bited Mommy," he said. He looked at the tree while opening and closing a small fist to the pulsing of the lights, and then underneath, at the shaggy cotton skirt without any presents on it.

In a calm voice I said, "I bet old Ginger's up there wagging that tail of hers. Did she used to wag her tail?" He looked at me with all his flat little teeth showing in his smile. "Here," I said, taking his hand in a shake, a modest up-and-down with light but steady pressure. I was teaching this to him. "That's the way," I said. And I thought about his father then, the man Tommy may have resembled, who through jealousy or greed or something worse had lost his family and a future worth believing in.

When Carol came in and stood by the television the snow beast was toothless and unoffending as a lamb. She looked around the room. "I'm mixed up with a couple of crazies," she said, and

Tommy laughed and said, "Crazies." Carol gathered the fallen cards and set them back. "I thought I was getting a cold before," she said. Her eyes were pink-rimmed and a little swollen, though she may have been smoking in her room. Without thinking I told her she looked run-down.

"I guess my prom queen days are behind me now," she said and smiled in her surprising way. She picked the throw pillow off the floor and sat between us. Tommy crawled half into her lap and she tousled his hair. "And you've got a voice that could drop a mountain, mister," she said and made him laugh squeezing at his sides. "God, Mommy. Oh God, Mommy," he said.

I finished my beer and went into the kitchen for another, and one for Carol. I thought about running out for another stringer, but the snow was leaning in against the sink window, and I watched a primered Formula inch up the winding hill. Police sirens began, weakly as though they were in my head, then peaked in wide rolling pulses. A few blocks in the direction of Father Panik Village they dropped off, and I stood there a minute feeling removed from the cold city.

Tommy was riled again when I joined them on the sofa, and I don't know, it had an effect on me. His frenzy now, dancing beside his mother, his hand gripping at her shoulder, wasn't any less enthusiastic than his frenzy before, with me. "There's that caterpillar," he said at another commercial. "If you have him you could walk him like a doggy. I knew it. I knew that was him." When his foot got caught between the cushions, Tommy lunged forward, tearing the gold chain from Carol's neck. I thrust an arm between his head and the coffee table just as Carol pulled him back into her lap. My beer foamed over the can and I hopped up. "Shit." I scraped icy lather from my jeans onto the braided rug. Tommy laughed. "I bet Santa's not laughing," I said. "You know what bad kids get?"

Tommy froze, and then his eyes moved and shone like melted ice. "I *am* a good boy," he said. "We're running away and not you,

Jerry. You don't get to." He opened his arms to his mother, who for a second was too busy giving me the stink eye to notice. Then she looked down at Tommy and softened. "Santa has your toys already made and ready, don't worry," she said. She began rocking slightly. "I promise."

"Look," I said, feeling a sudden crush of loneliness when Tommy said something in her ear, and she nodded and whispered something back.

"That was out of line," I said. "I apologize to both of you."

"It's by your foot," Carol said. I scooped the small gold cross from her necklace off the rug and handed it to her. "Listen to this one," I told Tommy. He hesitated and finally loosened from his mother, and I took a sec to remember things right. I told him about the time my father's Christmas present to me was two fifty-cent pieces. Only the way he did it was he put them in a small box, then that one in a bigger one, on and on. He handed me a package the size of a Tyco racing set. Smaller and smaller I went, tearing the boxes open in a rage, and my father had been drinking and thought it was the funniest thing ever. "So there I am," I said, "all these boxes around me and a buck to show for it." I took a long sip of my beer, and Carol shook her head in a pleasing way that said I was forgiven.

But Tommy stared at me, his mouth agape. "It was just a gag," I said. "A joke." He crawled over Carol, got to his feet and touched me on the shoulder. His eyes found mine and waited there as if he didn't know how to tell me something awful. "But when," he said.

"I was a kid. Little."

He slapped a hand at the air between us. "When did he give you the race cars?"

Carol and I were out on her porch having cigarettes when the subject of Tommy's father came up. We were just talking, one thing to the next. The stars were out and it was cold as hell. Between triple-decker houses a breeze made your cigarette glow red.

"They'd race in the desert for money, pink slips, whatever," she said. "Chevys only. Fords and Mopars were the antichrist."

"Was his name Tom?"

"Rick. That's Tommy's first name. Richard Thomas." She rubbed her arm, and a small bouquet of sparks shot off her Winston. "He gave me this tattoo," she said, pointing her chin to where it was under her jeans. "The gift you can't return."

Leaning against the railing I tore strings of wood from a rotted baluster, thinking about him scribbling that sloppy mark like a mutt staining its territory. I took a few long drags of my cigarette. "He race pro?"

She smoothed a pouch under her eye and shook her head. "Just out to strips in the desert. You felt sorry for those poor cars. They were like abused pets. You could smell them burning up, oil or rubber, that kind of smell. Like any minute it would all just explode."

"He sounds like a winner." I imagined him in a bandanna cap and Harley-patched leathers, someone probably cut from free weights and maybe hitting the bag, quiet around men but intense. Someone, though, who had limitations like anyone else on God's green earth. What keeps a man from acting out of his dignity is knowing this when the dangerous moment finally comes. "Sounds like a real boy scout," I said, the skin of my throat coppery in the thin air.

She shrugged and dropped her shoulders. "Life had a different set of rules then," she said. Nearby a door slammed and a woman with a cracking voice called, "Jessie! Jessica!" into the night. Carol turned toward the sound, which was coming from an old brick apartment complex across the street. The calling ended. Between rooftops a patch of stars hung upon us like chips of ice. Then Carol turned to me and said, "Do you think it's funny the way I'm raising him? Peculiar I mean. Do I raise him in a way that's peculiar?"

It wasn't something I'd given much thought to, and I told her I didn't think so. I flicked my cigarette into the street. "Let's go back inside," I said.

Carol scooped her hair back with one hand so that her face seemed narrow and drawn, and she paused, watching me watch her. "Sometimes you worry about our ages, don't you, Jerry. You worry it'll reach a point where you won't find me attractive and you won't be able to say it."

"Jesus, Carol."

She ground her cigarette into the scabby paint of the porch floor. "You should know that I'm brazen to that," she said, "to that and about anything else you could throw at me. I don't get petty about things. And if you were seeing someone else right now, that would be all right, too."

"What the hell does that mean?"

"I never asked for commitment, Jerry," she said. "Just even-temperedness." She pulled her hands back in the cuffs of her jacket, and the funny thing was that right then she looked younger to me. Girlish. She looked like someone I'd never met.

I went back inside. Tommy was belly-down in front of the TV, cheeks on palms on elbows. I had on the Brotherhood of the Right silk-screened jacket I'd won off a retired member in a card game, and Tommy turned to watch me take it off. He liked the smell of leather, and I knew he wanted to wear it. "What?" I said, and without looking at me again he got off the floor and ran toward his room. "I'm not in a mood," I said after him. His door slammed. "I'm not in any goddamn mood." I threw the jacket on the couch and went into the bathroom.

The exhaust fan droned as I paced and finally opened the medicine cabinet over the sink. I didn't know what I was doing. There was Mint Flavored Fluoride Gel, Band Aids that said Adhesive Strips for Cuts and Scrapes. There was a prescription bottle on the top shelf. Tranxene, it said, with NO REFILL typed under her name, and I could judge by its weight that it was almost empty. And two things suddenly came to my attention: I'd been lining the cabinet's contents on the edge of the sink, and Carol was standing at the open door.

She took the bottle from me, knocked one of the blue pills onto her palm and brought it to her mouth. "I wonder," she said, opening her eyes from swallowing, "if that day at your shop I should have just paid for the brake job and drove away clean. Or maybe I should have told you I needed love in small increments."

"I didn't deserve that," I said. I couldn't remember when words like these had become possible and even necessary to me. I folded my arms and looked at the brown grout between the tiles. "Seeing someone else."

"You didn't." She closed the door behind her as if she had some further action in mind, but she seemed to lose purpose. Her hands found her front pockets and she sighed. "I waitressed at a truck stop for four years," she said. "That was the rock bottom of my life. And what I remember is that you won't spill coffee if you don't watch yourself carrying it. Isn't that a telling thing? Four years of my life, and that's what I can show for it." She looked at me, and I realized I'd been waiting for her to. She opened her arms. "Will you please come over here?"

Four days before Christmas Carol was making dinner for us. I'd come over late, and Tommy had already eaten. He was sleeping in the living room, which was pretty much the routine, as was her carrying him to bed while I set up a movie. Some nights she would stay with him for half an hour. I'd get up and start walking toward the door, to peek in on what was happening, but the hallway floorboards creaked like crazy. I'd soft-foot back to the sofa and wait it out.

As Carol shook chicken legs in a baggy, I sat at the table with torn-out pages of K-Mart and Bradlees circulars strewn around me. I had an assignment. She'd circled pictures of toys—a talking Barney doll, a preschool tape recorder, that sort of thing—and my job was to cut out each picture with scissors. She planned to leave them under the tree Christmas morning for Tommy to find with notes from Santa. The next day they'd take the clippings to after-Christmas sales and get everything half price or better.

We were in the middle of dinner when the phone rang. Carol answered and thanked the other person for returning her call. She brought the phone to the counter by the sink and went through her purse. When she found her credit card she read the numbers out loud, and then she said what I assumed to be her mother's maiden name—the security code for inquires. "Who did?" she said. "Well, where did you send the bill? The address." Then she was still and quiet for a minute or more, and I set down my fork and walked up behind her. The phone receiver shook slightly in her hand, and her thumb pressed against the button to end the connection. She set the receiver down on the counter.

"Rick?" I said.

Carol faced the kitchen windows that against the night had become mirrors. "He had my bills sent to him," she said and turned on the sink faucet. "Jesus, what an idiot thing. I should have known he would have taken down my card numbers." The water started running out of the pot, taking all the soap with it, but she didn't shut it off.

"So he knows the state you live in now," I said, thinking through it. "Maybe the town. Where you shop." The phone started buzzing, and I hung it up. "All right. We're just going to wait and see what happens. I'll run home and pack some clothes. You bolt the door when I go."

I waited for a reaction from Carol because I was excited then and felt this development would connect us in a positive way. In the window reflection I could see the strange white of her eyes as she looked down into the sink. I grew aware of a coolness spreading through my upper body. Suddenly it was easy to think in terms of violence. "He won't stop if he thinks he can get away with it," I said.

"I don't need a hero's trouble, Jerry."

I went back to the table and slammed my chair. Still holding its back I saw the tendons in my wrist swollen like wires. "So now I'm the bad guy."

"Maybe I don't understand you," Carol said, turning from the sink, looking at me point blank. "Maybe you'd know just what to do if he found you here. I guess it doesn't matter." She crossed her arms and after a few moments let go of a breath. "I heard Tommy tell you about Ginger the other night. Half of Bridgeport heard."

"The fucker poisoned your dog. There you go."

"It wasn't antifreeze," she said. "Rick hung Ginger by the throat off a garage rafter because she bit me. I was the one who told him to get rid of her. Me." She shook her head and sniffed sharply, as though she'd been near tears. "I married him once. I used to love him, and I was a monster myself. That's what I have to live with. You're not a part of that."

"Listen to me, Carol. Someone's got to teach the son of a bitch what he is."

Carol pinched the bridge of her nose. She closed her eyes and slowly opened them. "I'll run," she said, in a voice flat with resolve. "If it comes down to that we'll run." She looked at the doorway and Tommy appeared. It was as if she knew his mind.

I went over to him as he squinted at the kitchen light. "We need a couple minutes," I said. His eyes were shiny and small and he didn't move. "Go on, now," I said.

Tommy touched the helmets on his 49er pajama bottoms, and there was a dark triangle of wet down his leg. "It's warm, Mommy," he said.

"Terrific," I said. "Just goddamn terrific."

"Let's get you in the bathroom," Carol said, and she turned off the sink water. "I'll be there in a minute." Tommy did what he was told, and when he was out of the room Carol said, "I want you to leave."

"Nobody's leaving."

"Don't turn this into anything tonight, or I'll hate you."

"Listen to me. He's a stalker for all I know. He'll break in a window."

"Don't make me hate you, Jerry."

I knocked over a chair and swore as it crashed. I grabbed my jacket in the living room, pausing just short of the door. Carol had followed, stopping as I did, ticking her nails once over the television, and in her face I could see that she was only there to make sure, to throw the bolt behind me. And taking the knob then, I felt the way you do in a plane lifting off, when you're between gravities and no one can tell you what will happen. As I stepped out into the steel slap of winter I promised myself it was over. I'd had enough.

Christmas fell on a Wednesday that year, and at noon when I pulled myself out of bed it could have as easily been any other day. I mailed a late card off to my mother and her husband in Florida. Nothing but church services on TV. I drank to Jesus, and I drank to Mary. I drank to the doughy, black-bearded priest who warned against losing faith in the New Year. Outside the air was damp and rotten with the Sound at low tide, and I walked the block over to the Reckloose. Behind the bar Dex was eating soup out of a can, and his face went blank when he saw me. Dex had been to prison in New Haven for stealing a snow-blower, a felony in the eyes of the law but not enough of a crime to afford him respect from the rest of us.

There wasn't anyone else in the bar I could see. "Somebody forgot to deck your halls," I said. He set his soup can on the bar and aimed his good leg in my direction, followed by a dragging bad leg. As he neared something took shape along his jaw, tobacco or food, but when he was right before me I saw it was four black stitches. "Who won?"

He shook his head. "With the pool cues, last night. Christmas friggin' eve." Then he cracked a Heineken under the counter and dropped it in front of me. "Where the hell you been?"

One night I drove out to Carol's. The streetlight coned out over her front porch, but the living room was dark. I parked two houses up and listened to the engine tick cool. I looked through my cassettes, straightened the glove box. I waited for inspiration.

I didn't need a black knit hat and shoe polish to sneak behind the place. There were no stars or moon. I looked first in her bedroom window. All the golf balls were gathered in the plastic cup. Empty boxes from grocery stores were stacked against the closet by her dresser, and her bed was made and empty. I tried to imagine us in there, holding each other, and when the vision came to me a cold space opened in my chest. I moved on, through an elm sapling brittle as toothpicks. Tommy's room was visible in an orange tent of nightlight, and in that soft place he slept with an arm slung loosely over his new Barney doll. Carol knelt by his bed with her hands laced at his feet. In a moment she looked across at him and her lips formed words I couldn't make out, words, I thought, that I had never heard her speak. And if she had cheated or had been otherwise to blame, it would have been all right with me then. I wanted to feel wronged and better for how things had turned, but the truth I couldn't get away from was that in some important way I had only proven myself insufficient. She dropped her face a little closer to her hands, and I stayed watching until my breath misted everything away.

I went back out front to her Citation and wormed my fingers in through the grille. I found the plastic-coated cable, traced it up to where bare wire was exposed, and pulled. The hood popped up to the latch. I didn't know exactly what I wanted to come of crossing her ignition wires. I thought maybe she would call me at the shop the next morning, and that was the best I could hope for.

When I clicked the hood down Carol was on her front porch

with a cigarette. She didn't look surprised to see me. She must have been there a while without letting on.

"I hope you didn't mess it up too bad under there."

"I'll go fix it," I said, but instead walked toward her. "Where are you going?"

"Key Largo if anyone asks," she said, "or Madagascar." She dragged on her cigarette and shook her head. "I'm not sure we're even going yet. It seems like a smart thing to be ready if I have to." She stabbed her cigarette against the door frame and flicked it away. "I'm not going to ask you in tonight, Jerry. So you might as well get any of those ideas out of your head. But I've got something for you."

She went inside, and I stayed on the porch. I wished there was a present in my car I could give her. I'd bought a pair of women's cabretta leather golf gloves but returned them the day after Christmas. That was all the shopping I'd done. When she came back out she handed me a card, its width the closest we'd come to touching in eight days. It was homemade out of heavy red paper. Inside was a crayon drawing of a blue-haired man in a leather jacket standing by a Christmas tree.

"He made a bunch of them," she said. "That one surprised me."

"I didn't bring his present," I said.

She pulled opened the door and stepped through. "I'll tell him you got the card."

The door closed and I was alone with my steaming breath under the streetlight. I looked at the card again. The tree held three different crayons' worth of ornaments. In the picture I was smiling.

All That Can Be Said

FOOTSTEPS UNDO THE FRAGILE QUIET. THEY ECHO BETWEEN plaster walls and continue past the composition office by the water fountain, the poetry office next door. Those feet are coming for me.

On the other side of my door the tempo ends, the student perhaps thumbing a touch screen or getting his nerve. My senses dilate like the man who wakes with an intruder downstairs. It's been only forty minutes between classes, but I've immersed myself, completely and unexpectedly, in a scene of my novel. Two years later, when the book is published, reviewers will capitalize on car metaphors: high-octane drama; tricked-out prose; a great American novel just pulled up. It's because I've been so deep in the mind of my protagonist, an eighteen-year-old repair mechanic, that I feel suddenly disoriented here in my tiny office packed with books.

Waiting on the knock I think, Be a teacher, though for a second my mind resists, as if I've told myself to be a neurosurgeon or a tree, and allows the other voice, the familiar one that asks who the hell I think I'm fooling.

An east coast city three time zones away, sixteen years earlier. I'm standing at the peg hooks reading the words "Police Auction Car" on a hanging work order. The last one was a Cadillac low-rider whose interior had been gutted for a contraband search. The ignitions are usually hammered out, the seats cut-up, wires hanging over your feet. And you never know what kind of nightmare is waiting under the hood—a high-compression three-fifty jammed in where you and the on-board computer are expecting a V-6.

I'm skimming the work order for a third time when Doug snatches it off the peg hooks. "Pussy," he says.

It's the end of the summer and slow. If the shop owner catches you bumming around he'll send you home, so I go over to Doug's bay and try to look busy. The auction car is a Smokey and the Bandit TransAm with T-tops and a honeycomb grille. Doug looks asleep on his feet as he drops the vinyl mats over its deep black fenders. He coughs and can't seem to clear his throat. At twenty-two he has a grizzled look, his face doughy and bloodless, especially in the morning. I'm three years younger and can't imagine being his age. The difference between us is that he's lived his whole life in Waterbury, whereas I've moved every two or three years with my divorced mother and still have faith that things can change.

I see through the driver's window that the stereo has been yanked and is, for some reason, sitting on the passenger floor. You never know with these police auction cars. Some have been in shoot-outs. Once I had a GT Mustang with pink smears on the headliner where they'd tried to clean off blood.

"Any bullet holes?" I say.

Doug squints at the nose spoiler as he lights a Winston. I light one, too, and try to mimic his cool demeanor. You have to stay focused around spinning fan blades and scorching manifolds. It's like that kid's game Operation, only touching metal means a whole lot of pain.

But it's good work for Waterbury, which is like a looted city with the old brass mills caving in, the Victorian mansions diced up into section 8 apartments. Unemployment is at 11% and a lot of guys have to wear hair nets after high school. At the shop we get paid to unravel engine problems all day, and you can smoke and cuss and bang your head to Metallica. The roach coach rolls in at 12:20 with a menu range from grilled cheese on up to beef stroganoff.

Doug corrals the oscilloscope leads in his blackened hands and swings around the boom arm. The TransAm has a 6.6 liter with a Shaker air cleaner that Doug leaves assembled while he runs the first few tests. Timing. Cylinder balance. The low KV spikes indicate carbon fouled spark plugs, and the CO and HC levels soar when Doug brings up the idle. The engine hits a flat spot and starts to cough. It's getting too much fuel, or not enough air. A sticking float or choke—I'm already adding the job up in my head. If you fix a problem, the shop owner expects you to double the estimate with extra services—tune up, oil change, maybe a wire set or a coolant flush—and we make a small commission on top of the hourly wage. Doug might be looking at a $500 ticket, which is just about what I did in ten hours yesterday.

I lean over the fender mat and unscrew the wing nut from the air cleaner. The idle smoothes out when I take off the cover. "Lucky bastard," I say. It's just a clogged air filter, cheese ball commish.

Doug lifts out the filter with a grunt. "Fuck. Feel that thing." It has to be a few pounds. I give it back and he holds it up to the florescent lights, trying to see through the accordion paper. On one of the rolling parts trays he tears into it with a pair of dikes, looking pissed and determined, then confused.

It isn't actually an air filter. Under wire mesh on the bottom they've used foil-wrapped cardboard as a heat shield. Stacked along the inside of the filter are four long balloons, the kind they twist into animals at the fair. A heavy staple clamps shut the open ends, and I can see that they're really three balloons, one inside the other.

"Wait a minute," Doug says. "See it? Hang on." He chews a blackened thumb nail. "They got the open side facing the air intake. Smart. The other way, the motor wouldn't even idle. Mastermind, bro." He takes a box cutter from one of the small top drawers of his tool box.

I can't believe the cops missed it, even with the drug-sniffing dogs. And then for a minute my brain stops holding thoughts all together. I know what it is—I've seen every season of *Miami Vice*— but I can't let myself form the words. There is a door behind me that is my life so far, and what this is closes that door.

Doug makes a slice in the rubber. A gap opens like lips on a sleepy mouth, and the powder spills out. On the blackened mat it is bright as snow in sunshine. It glistens and is precious. I wonder in a panicked moment if we're under surveillance. "Don't touch it," I say.

Doug dips his dirty fingertip in and brings it up to taste. His eyes, that are always just slits, that I didn't think could be made wide, bulge out when the finger touches the tongue. "That's a shitload of money," he says. He closes over the slice he's made with electric tape. Half a thimble full has spilled out. Between two fingers and a thumb he pinches it up and releases it into the palm of the other hand. He glances around the bay, at the parts room, the lobby door. "Stay here. I'm going to find out for sure." As fast as I've ever seen him do anything he breaks past the dynamometers into the locker room. I hear the bathroom door in there close and lock.

My cleanest finger I drag through what's left on the mat, my jaw shaking. It's like Orajel on my tongue, and then bitter, and I spit out the wash of saliva. Bars and package stores in Waterbury have been serving me for two years, but as for drugs I've never done more than pot, not necessarily by choice but because anything stronger is never where I happen to be. And now I'm touching this strange, volatile dust of a new world.

Doug storms back, takes away the packages and before I can speak is out getting into his Corolla. He hits Wolcott Avenue with a chirp of rubber.

I go in the parts room and take down eight Bosch spark plugs. On the fender mats of the TransAm I carefully gap them. I needed to count, so I count my breaths. It may be my first experience with meditation. When it doesn't work I go in the alley between our shop and Firestone and tear the filter off a Marlboro that I smoke so fast I raise two little blisters between my fingers. I light another.

Then I hear the rusted-out muffler as he swings back in the lot and parks.

He's done a very stupid thing. He's taken the balloons to Save-A-Lot and weighed them on a fruit scale. "A little over two pounds," he says. "We're loaded, bro." He paces along the TransAm and grins with new life breathed into him. I've been drunk and stoned with him maybe a dozen times, and have seen his gloominess only deepen, but I don't know what happens to him on harder drugs.

Or maybe it's more than the coke he's snorted.

He says we can get ten thousand. "Ten easy," he says.

I don't ask him how he knows. We buy our weed from a college guy who comes in for oil changes, and I assume Doug knows about other drugs the same way I do, from TV.

He has a plan: Tonight we'll find a hooker on Cherry Street. We'll give her some in an envelope to take to her pimp. We'll offer him two hundred dollars just for connecting us with a dealer who can buy it all.

Later, Doug is certain we'll get twelve for it, six each—it's money in the bank. I've never had close to that amount saved up, and two days earlier I saw a '70 SS Chevelle in Hemmings Motor News for $6,500. As soon as I let myself imagine lighting the tires in that ride, I'm in.

I'm not sure what the money means to Doug. I know that Cindy moved out. They dated since high school, and she's hot, and likely to be his last hot girlfriend since he's getting fat and already losing his hair. Under magnets on his refrigerator are pictures of them at the prom and other places. It's a different Doug with thick, feathered hair and no stubble, smiling as if he were high. In two pictures he's playing an electric blue Stratocaster.

Cindy is living with one of her friends. Most of her stuff is already out of the apartment. I don't know how this money will change any of that for Doug, but at the peg hooks he takes down the board for a transverse V-8 Cadillac, whose back spark plugs you have to be a double-jointed contortionist to change, and I hear him singing Judas Priest as he approaches the saddle-brown monstrosity with a seat cover and floor mat. Even when I first met him, and he still played guitar and was still sleeping with Cindy, he wasn't happy like this.

After lunch I run across the street to People's Bank to take out $100, which leaves me $418 in my savings account. Doug gets $100 from his bank, and I don't know how much he has left. When he leans over the skipping Ford Matador I'm working on, we talk about how incompetent the police who searched the car are. Maybe the dogs didn't smell it in the engine compartment—if they bothered to use dogs—but all they had to do was unscrew a wing nut. And it feels good to insult them. It makes what we're talking about doing seem reasonable. We didn't smuggle it from Columbia, or where ever. We didn't threaten or kill anyone. And if the cops had just done their job, we never would have found it.

This is the kind of neighborhood Cherry Street runs through: Once a guy robbing a liquor store was hit in the neck by a stray bullet from another robbery across the street.

Doug is in my passenger seat. On the west side in the dark is a five story brick building with all its windows broken out. The glowing heads of cigarettes drift around inside. I pull over in front of an overgrown lot with people standing around as if waiting for a rally or a concert to start. The hooker who walks up to Doug's window barely speaks English. She's pretty and our age, wearing shimmer eye shadow and a gallon of Poison. "What you want?" she keeps saying. When we stammer and stall she thinks it's funny. She thinks we're shy.

Doug gives her the envelope as I turn on the interior light. She looks in but won't touch the big pinch of coke at the bottom. She glances at me like it's the last thing she expected. She says something in Spanish and for a second looks afraid. I see a glimpse of her younger, before men, and try to believe neither of us belongs here. I can't make myself say, "Pimp," so I say, "We want to sell it. We have a lot to sell."

I haven't finished speaking before she turns and is gone. I watch her in Doug's side mirror, and she stops in the rim of a lone street light. She looks around and is smoking a cigarette, and after a long minute, when I hear myself asking, "What the fuck," over and over, an enormous black man in a Giants jersey appears next to her. Doug leans forward to see in the side mirror, so I have to turn around and look through the back window. The guy is holding the envelope and talking to the girl. He laughs. "He doesn't want it," I say.

"Wait," Doug says.

She hands him her cigarette, which he finishes and steps out. He begins walking toward us, and what scares me most is that she stays behind. Another man jogs up and joins the big man, and I face forward and slam the shifter into first. Doug turns, and like siblings listening to their parents fight we plead silently for peace in the weak dome light. I look in his mirror. They're in the blind spot or coming around to my side.

I don't look at Doug again. I gun it and tear the fuck out of there.

A guy that I'm sure has a gun crosses the street very slowly. In opposition to my urgency, he all but stops in front of me. When I swerve around him there is a thump that I think is the sound of a foot being run over, but in my mirror he is standing with his leg swinging back from having kicked a dent the size of a coffee can in the quarter panel.

I turn onto High, then Orange, then Vine. There are no headlights anywhere, there is no sound, and in the calm I feel a shaky second of pride that we've done all we are capable of. At least we tried. No one else would have gone this far. Doug must feel the same because he lets me grab the balloons from the flip-lid compartment and throw them out the window. The liberation sends a shock of giddiness through my gut, though tonight I'll lie awake wondering if the police have somehow gotten our finger prints off of them.

Doug isn't mad at me. He seems to be taking the whole misadventure as more evidence that his dreams will forever be just out of reach. "Man," he says. That is all, and that is everything. If a single word can express more disenchantment, I haven't heard it.

Doug's apartment is in a long level of pebble-stuccoed rectangles, a narrow concrete landing in front of each door. I pull up and turn off the headlights.

"He wasn't going to buy it," I say, and the words cause blood to surge from my arms and legs into my heart. "He thought we were punks."

Doug puts a cigarette on his lip. He pushes my dashboard lighter and settles back, looking at his dark apartment. "She's staying with that lesbo Carmen," he says. The lighter pops, but he ignores it. "Fucking head cases," he says. "They deserve each other. I tell you what I did to her car?"

I just want to be in my apartment. I want to get my handgun from the sock drawer and tell myself I'm safe.

Doug doesn't say what he did to her car. "There's Absolut in the freezer," he says.

"Not tonight."

He nods, the cigarette still unlit on his lip. It's what he expected to hear. After a while he opens the door, and the light hurts our eyes. "Write if you find work," he says, which is sometimes how we say goodbye. But then he takes another step and swings around. "I'm getting out of this fucking town."

"Yeah," I say, not sure if I'm now complicit in his plans, and not really caring.

In less than a month there will be an electrical fire in his kitchen. They'll say it started in the pop-up toaster, where he was always lighting cigarettes. It won't be from burns but smoke inhalation. He may have been drunk or high, or he may have opened his eyes but couldn't summon the will to leave the room that would become his mausoleum. He never got off the couch.

At the funeral service family and friends will weep at the lectern, some committing his death to the will of God, some laboring to assign his short life meaning. As I listen my blood will race with dark and unfamiliar rage that drives me out of the sanctuary, but not out of the shop bays, not for another five years.

Between classes I stare at the Italian Renaissance arcade outside my office window and wonder what the crew from Waterbury would make of me now. In a simple world the speculating would end with a warm appreciation of the journey, perhaps a smug grin. But too often I'm left feeling anxious, regretting the six years after high school that passed without reading a book or writing more than a few sentences on a work order.

In the end, the student knocked on my office door and now sits across from me on an old trestle chair. How often I've envied my students their breeziness, their entitled sense of being exactly where they belong, but in this young man's eyes I see the unutterable yearning that shepherded us to Cherry Street all those years ago. Slumped forward, he clamps his hands in hard prayer.

The problem? He missed his short story workshop. After a few attempts at an opening word—"So," "Look," "Okay"—he says, "The guy everyone's…that student Monday…" but sour chords strain his voice, and he starts again. "The sophomore who shot himself, we were friends."

Words often fail me. On campus, I take pains to sound like someone whose legitimacy here is beyond reproach. The word that comes to me now is one I might say to pander, to sound hip, so I've banned myself from using it around students. But as I look at this young man, who is the age I was when I would have taken six thousand dollars over a college degree any day of the week, I feel only his pain. "Man," I say.

He looks up at me, and that word is enough. It is, in fact, all that can be said, and the quiet that I intuitively avoid with students is suddenly corrective, a kinship that contains loss and wisdom more profound than I can quote him from any book. For a moment I smell the sinus-searing brake cleaner on hot metal, mineral spirits in the soak tank, tailpipe hydrocarbons and gasoline—always gasoline—in thick pockets all around the shop.

The Wreck

MIKE BOYLE DROVE WITH A LIGHT FOOT, HOPING THE STIFF suspension might jounce Connor to sleep, but no luck tonight. His son sat forward wide awake on the wrecker's bench seat, tracking porch lights through the small river town. As the roadway opened a temporary third lane Connor suddenly lunged at Boyle and fell back. "Let me drive," he said in his grunting way.

"Oh, you think so?"

"I can drive no problem."

"And what do I tell the statie that pulls us over?"

"Flies in the buttermilk," Connor said, grinding one fist into the other. "Flies in the buttermilk shoo fly shoo."

It was a second childhood for Connor, and whereas Boyle had been absent for much of the first one, he now helped with feedings and baths, dressing routines and trips to bed. This time around there would be no illusions of Connor outgrowing his breathless sentences and clunky gestures. Dr. Messner called it a miracle that Connor had come even this far.

Boyle patted around the seat for his cigarettes as the stout truck nearly drove itself. "Go ahead and play the radio," he said, "but that window stays up tonight. Got me? Don't worry about what I'm doing." A wheel-lift job would have been one thing, but tonight the call had been for the Hino, the big diesel slide-tray that scraped up demolished cars like a giant spatula. "It's not a breakdown like last time," Boyle said.

Connor wasn't listening. Boyle saw that he had the top flipped back on the pack of Winstons.

"Where'd you get those? Here. Thank you. Can I have them?"

Connor feinted handing the pack over, then pulled it back, feinted again. Boyle glanced at the road only long enough to keep off the lines and then back at Connor, who wasn't jerking the cigarettes, whose hand wasn't shaking, or was shaking less. Then Connor pitched forward and mashed his other hand into his groin. "Dad," he said. "Hey Dad."

"You need to go?" Boyle clicked on the signal light. They were a quarter-mile from the turnoff for Leaburg Dam, where there were chemical toilets on the street-side bank above the fish ladder. He parked near a stock pond of steelhead and white sturgeon, big hungry fish that would boil the water for pellets you could buy from a gumball machine.

Boyle hopped out of the truck and lit up the gravel grade to the pair of teal Honey Buckets. He propped a trash barrel against the door of one and raced back down to the truck, yelling over the spillway water that crashed to froth at the base of the dam: "You just count to five for me, son. Hang tight!"

His son's legs shuddered as Boyle swung them around to the edge of the bench seat. Connor had lost twenty pounds since the wreck, but the sudden heft of him pumped lightning up Boyle's spine as he loaded him piggy-back and staggered up the hill. Just as he got the boxers down the hot piss sprayed Boyle's stomach before he could aim it down the plastic hole. Boyle fell back against the toilet paper rail open-mouthed to catch his breath.

From the open door of the truck Freddy Sterling's voice boomed over the CB radio. "Big Man, where you at?" Boyle couldn't go down to answer or talk or do anything other than breathe.

Connor stared out the door space at the big moon-flecked river. After a minute he said, "Steelhead."

Boyle rubbed a fist-size wad of tissue over his shirt and used hand sanitizer to cut the smell. "That's right," he said.

"I got five big ones."

"You got one, and Shorty Burke got one. I got blanked."

"Mine was the lunker," Connor said. He'd been, Boyle remembered, hung over that morning from running around with Ed Mancini and that bunch all night. At seventeen Connor was mouthy and bullheaded, but when he hooked into that chrome twelve-pound hen and steered her hard out of the chute all the way up to Shorty's net, he was giddy as a boy. "Dad, what's she weigh?" he said. "What do you think?"

Boyle worked his way down to the truck, Connor's arms in a fireman hold around his neck, his feet dragging on the loose gravel. After Connor was snapped in his seatbelt, Boyle picked up the radio receiver. "What's up, Freddy?"

"Christ, I'm going bat-shit over here. Ten minutes I'm trying to get you."

Boyle pulled back onto the McKenzie Highway as Freddy complained. Twice already the cop on the scene had called in to find out where the truck was.

"Tell him I'm obeying the county speed limit," Boyle said. "Just now passing Leaburg –"

"Fat Freddy," Connor yelled before Boyle could flip his thumb off the receiver. In the radio silence that followed, Boyle doubted Freddy had understood—Connor talked like his mouth was full of bread.

"You got Connor out this late?" Freddy said.

"No choice. That cop calls back, I'm fifteen minutes away." Boyle started to hang up the receiver but then brought it back. "Freddy, they say what happened?"

"Booze and brains, sounds like. One car roll-over."

"Booze and brains," Connor started hollering until Boyle told him to pipe down. Boyle stared at the roadway ahead, clouds of gnats breaking up in the headlights, to where the fir trees started past town. It was a bonehead notion to think he could bring Connor along on a Hino job. He and Joyce needed the money, but they'd run on fumes before and always found a way. He braked into the first dirt turnaround and picked up the receiver.

"Freddy," he said, "I can't do it tonight. I'm sorry."

"Come again. Over."

"You heard what I said. Who else you got?"

"Farwell and Davich are up at the track. You're who I got. Listen, Mike. You want F&M to get the statie account? I'm in a freaking bind here."

Boyle took a moment and lowered his voice. "I don't want my boy to have to see something."

No answer, and Boyle was just hanging up the receiver when Freddy said, "Something like what?"

"A B-O-D-Y."

"Listen to me, Mike—"

"Sorry, Freddy." He replaced the receiver and shut off the radio as Connor stared intently at the roadway ahead. The soft dashboard light veiled Connor's scars in shadow, and Boyle—just for a second or two—let himself slip into the fantasy that Connor was well. The heat was building through Boyle's sinuses. Connor stayed focused and still, but Boyle didn't look outside because he knew, after having chased Connor's gazes before, that nothing would be there. "Let's head home," Boyle said, just as Connor's forehead shimmered fiery red. Boyle turned to see the ambulance crest, its sirens cut off between intersections, and come at them fast.

"You saw the lights?" Boyle said. "Up in the trees?"

"Here it goes," Connor said, slicing at the air, laughing.

Boyle extended the EMTs a steering wheel wave as the Hino trembled in its wake. When he turned on the radio Freddy was yelling, and he brought up the receiver again. "The ambulance that just passed," Boyle said. "That them?"

"Yes. Goddamit. That's what I been telling you."

"Then I lied, Freddy," Boyle said. "We're on our way."

An overturned Mitsubishi Eclipse lay on the shoulder of the southbound lane, its hood and fenders outlined in hissing road flares. Connor stared at the car, the amber top lights of the Hino swimming across it, with his mouth over his hand and a knuckle in his teeth. He didn't remember his own wreck, but still Boyle watched to be sure that Connor's sympathetic amnesia—Dr. Messner's term—remained intact. "We'll have to winch it back over," Boyle said. "Freddy's looking at a fat check on this one."

"Cop," Connor said, watching the policeman who stood waiting by the grille of his state prowler.

Boyle got out and called back into the cab for his son not to touch anything. He hadn't seen Lester Rampardt in more than a year, and Rampardt came over with his hand out.

"Officer Rampardt on the case," Boyle said.

"I heard a rumor Mike Boyle was towing for Sterling's. Wasn't just the one job enough for you?"

"Not according to the folks at Master-Card." Boyle pulled a glove out of each front jacket pocket, the canvas stiff and shrunken from getting wet too many times.

"Well, hey," Rampardt said. "You got yourself a helper."

"Apprentice," Boyle said. "All this will be his someday."

Rampardt nodded, staring into the cab. "Is that right?"

Boyle smiled and immediately felt heavy. "I'm joking, Les. No, they're saying he's not going to walk again." In his chest came a small hitch he hadn't felt since his hangover days, when he'd realize that the night before, in the clamor of a loud bar, he'd mistreated a close friend. Now the moment surprised Boyle, who considered himself, at this point in life, well beyond caring about social blunders.

"Joyce pulled a graveyard at Weyerhaeuser," Boyle said. "She's got me on sitter duty tonight." He watched Rampardt, who wore the typical, uneasy look of someone not used to the sight of Connor: his dented forehead, his wall-eye, the crude palsied shake of his hands.

Boyle took out his Maglite, and they walked over to the Mitsubishi. The car looked like the end result of a movie stunt. Rampardt dug a can from the pocket of his collar shirt and said,

"You'll have to knock it back around somehow." He didn't avert his eyes as he tucked a pair of Skoal Bandits behind his lip.

Gloves and flashlight tucked under an arm, Boyle lit a cigarette. As the nicotine did its warm work they stared at the Eclipse as though at a campfire, the flares giving off a Fourth of July smell. Rampardt took off his patrolman's hat and held it pressed against his thigh. He didn't push his hand back through his hair, which was side-parted and years behind Boyle's in going gray, but he seemed to relax in the small luxury of exposing his forehead to the night. Watching him, Boyle felt a mild pressure headache begin to dissolve in the clean forest air. Then Rampardt cocked his head and had his first spit.

"How many in the car?" Boyle said.

"Just one."

"Drunk?"

Rampardt shrugged. "Jury's still out. She says no."

Under a big misshapen moon, Boyle looked down the twenty yards of roadway before the wreck. Dry as a garage floor and generally straight in both directions. He expected to share a laugh over her claim that she wasn't drunk, but Rampardt was staring gravely at the car. Its hood hung down from the engine compartment like the open mouth of a dog.

"She said a deer run across," Rampardt said.

Boyle aimed his flashlight over the guardrail. A narrow ledge fell off fifty feet to a boiling channel in the river. "One of Santa's reindeer, must'a been."

Rampardt set the patrolman's hat back on and straightened it. "Do me a favor, wise guy. Get this car picked up so we can go home." He grinned in a way that took Boyle back to a night more than thirty years ago. A week after graduating together from Springfield High, Boyle and Rampardt split a case of Olympias in the front seat of Boyle's Chevelle. "I'll probably buy it the minute I jump off the helicopter," Rampardt had said. "Step on a mine or something." But in his grin, there in the light of the car radio, Boyle saw Rampardt didn't believe what he was saying, and Boyle didn't believe it, either. Rampardt maneuvered through his life with an advantage that Boyle couldn't name, a clarity of purpose and a destiny to fulfill. Not by luck but by design, Rampardt would come home from Vietnam without a scratch.

From behind a dark outcropping in the distance, a pair of headlights appeared, small as buttons in the coiling fog. Rampardt turned on his flashlight. "There's a gas smell," he said to Boyle. "Watch your cigarette around the hood." He went out and rolled the flashlight up and down to slow the vehicle, a muddy four-by-four, and guide it past the wreck.

Boyle walked around to the other side of the car. He stepped out his cigarette and pulled on his work gloves, gripping the striped top canvas in his teeth as he pushed his fingers to the tips. A breeze grew steadily, flowing into the gorge from the west and smelling vaguely of the Pacific, as it sometimes did at night, though the ocean was more than an hour away. It was good to be out in the night air. Often in his sobriety, which was less than two years old—fledgling, as his AA sponsor called it—Boyle found himself appreciating sensations he once took for granted: the cool and warmth of the outdoors, the soothing white noise of moving water. He looked up at the pinpricked sky between bows of towering doug fir, feeling as if he were standing under the heavy furniture of giants.

Boyle turned from the breeze and zipped his jacket midway up his chest. He liked the idea of fall and then winter coming. He and Joyce would dress Connor in scarves, mittens, things he never would have worn himself but seemed not to mind now. When he'd been out of Sacred Heart only a few weeks, they'd pulled bright sweaters down over his head and said, "Hubba, hubba," and "Got a hot date?"

Though they'd kept the house warm, Connor caught pneumonia that first spring. One night Joyce came out to the back porch where Boyle was watching the sun set on a clear-cut behind the house, a half-gallon bottle of Seagram's on the picnic table in front of him. When she picked up the bottle, he didn't look up, didn't want to see the hurt on her face from standing at Connor's bedside listening to him wheeze.

"I'll get you a glass," he said and had just gotten up when the bottle exploded, chunks of glass ricocheting off concrete and a good quart of whiskey battering his pant legs. He grabbed her arm. "The hell, woman?"

Joyce said nothing, wrenching free of him and collapsing into the chair beside his.

"Don't you go quiet on me, now," he said.

She dropped her face into her hands. Quietly, watching her, Boyle eased back into his chair.

"Only Connor matters to me," she said. "Our friends can go to hell. This whole town, too. If we don't get our shit together, he's going to die. Someday we'll be out here, we'll be drinking and he'll hit his head or choke on a …" Joyce choked up herself, and when she covered her mouth and wept he was surprised to find how much he still loved her. He'd all but written them off as drinking buddies by then, but now he felt only a need to protect her, a hot welling inside him. He opened his arms, and for the first time in years she came and sat on his lap.

That night on their back porch she handed him a picture. It was of Connor in his hospital bed after all the bruises had gone green. His head was big and dented, his left eye shifted from the socket reconstruction, his skull wrapped thickly in cotton.

"Look at it the next time you want a drink," she said.

They were perpetually on the brink of bankrupt now, but they kept Connor out of the state-run group homes. They knew the stories—shit-smeared walls, rape, mismanaged medicine—and every day he was living at home brought them a clear victory. They were living without for their son.

Rampardt's voice interrupted his thoughts. "It's far enough off the road, I'd have let it keep till morning." Most of the car was clearly visible in the prowler's spotlight. "But I don't like a car upside-down. Fluids end up in the river and you'll have environmentalists looking to outlaw motor vehicles in general."

Out of the diamond plate toolbox, Boyle hefted fifty feet of choker chain he used to anchor the truck to a guardrail post. "She going to be okay, then?" he said. "The driver?"

"Broken wrist, maybe. A cut on her forehead." Rampardt looked at the car and shook his head. "She smelled that gas, and good night. Talk about a set of lungs. I reached in and held her hand, and we said the Lord's prayer together." He shook his lead, grinning. "Them EMTs looked at us like we was snake handlers."

Boyle shined the light in through where the driver's door was peeled backward like the foil on a baked potato. The cut lap and shoulder belts hung limply behind a spilled-out windshield, and the headliner was covered with glass pebbles and Dunkin' Donuts cups and college textbooks and ATM receipts and pens and pennies. It was a canvas bag with the Mona Lisa on the front that made Boyle think of Connor's old girlfriend, Jenny. Hers had a different painting, and though Boyle had seen it a thousand times on his kitchen table, and though she had carried it with her those few times she visited Connor after the wreck, Boyle couldn't remember what the painting was.

He pulled the big Clevis hook from the winch spool and looked for a solid section of frame with his flashlight. Even upside-down, the car looked much better than Connor's Monte Carlo had. Boyle himself was drinking at the Summit View that night, and he only saw the car at the salvage yard a week later. The engine had broken free on impact, coming to rest fifty yards from the car, and part of the hood had pierced the passenger seat. One morning, not long after Connor was talking again, he wheeled himself to the closet, opened the door himself somehow, and looked in the one mirror they had forgotten to take down, on the inside of the closet door.

"God," he said, touching his face. "God God God." Boyle couldn't stay in the room. Had the buckled metal gone a centimeter deeper, Connor would have been dead on the scene.

Bent over the wreck now, Boyle pushed at the undercarriage and set the hook on the center of the frame side rail. When a crackle from Rampardt's portable radio announced his presence behind him, Boyle turned. "I think she'll flip okay. Can't say how she'll pull up onto the bed."

Rampardt crouched to look in the car, and Boyle shone his flashlight around the interior. The gearshift looked to be in third or fifth; he'd have to knock it into neutral. There was a lump in the Mona Lisa bag, just a fleck of white glass under the edge stitching. A diesel mechanic for twenty-three years, Boyle kept a pocket-protector inside his jacket stocked with small screwdrivers, a Leatherman, a grease pencil, and now he took out a magnet on a telescopic handle.

As he protracted the antenna-like handle, Rampardt said, "What's that for?"

"Watch." Boyle reached in through the Jaws of Life tear in the driver's door and uncovered the bottle. Rampardt aimed his light in.

"Malibu rum," Boyle said, pulling back out of the car. "You figure she hid it like that on purpose?"

"Don't tell me Mike Boyle's playing detective, now."

Boyle chuckled.

"You certain you didn't drop that in there?" Rampardt said.

Boyle swung around but caught himself, breathing once before he spoke. "Les, is there some sort of grievance with me tonight?"

Rampardt didn't answer at first, and when he finally looked at Boyle his eyes seemed polished in the headlights of the truck. "Look. Do me a favor, Mike. Wait until her blood test comes back before you tell it around. I know this girl. Her and my Kimmy are at UO together."

Boyle watched him. He could have let it go, but something about Rampardt's tone got his blood up. "Who am I going to tell, Les? I got enough trouble."

"That Freddy Sterling has a big mouth," Rampardt said, and then both men jumped when the Hino's horn beeped. Boyle went back and opened the door, his son hollering inside. "I'll get it out of there if you let me," Boyle said.

"What's that he said?"

"He doesn't like the car being upside-down."

Rampardt looked in at Connor and nodded. "Me either, son."

Connor started hollering again. Boyle turned on the radio and went up through the presets. "You say when." He found an old rock song that settled Connor and then closed the door.

"I believe he just told me go to hell," Rampardt said. He opened his stance a little and brought his hands behind him. "Is that how you understood it?"

"He's tired. It's late."

"Yeah," Rampardt said. "That's not all of it." As he turned slightly to look down at the road, pits of acne scars on his jaw line filled with shadow in the moonlight. "No, he remembers me," he said. Late one night three years ago, Rampardt had brought Connor home after picking him up for fighting in a Carl's Jr. parking lot. "I'd guess he's about triple the legal limit," Rampardt had said. "See if you can get some food in him." It was a favor to Boyle that Rampardt didn't arrest Connor, but the favor was buried deep in a look of irritation, even disgust. Boyle, shit-faced himself after a blowout with Joyce, had the urge to tell Rampardt to get the hell off his property and take Connor with him. A night in lockup might teach the kid some sense. But in the end he just thanked Rampardt and followed Connor, staggering and cussing, up to the house.

"He remembers me," Rampardt said again. He dug out the tobacco pouches from his lip and flung them into the road.

Boyle looked at his son, who was staring off in the dark

listening to music. "Do me a favor, Les," he said. "Go shake his hand. See what he does."

"I don't think we'd better," Rampardt said. Something came over his portable radio, and he turned up the volume. He listened for a moment, staring at the twisted end of guardrail lying in the fireweed, and then turned it back down. He looked at his watch. "Okay. For real this time. Let's get this car off the road."

"Go on," Boyle said, but Rampardt brought his hands over his belt buckle and otherwise didn't move. Boyle stared at him. "All I'm asking is you shake my boy's hand."

"I said no, Mike. Now leave it alone."

"Go pray with him," Boyle said. "You can say prayers with Miss Malibu Rum out here. Go on, he'll listen. I'll get him to listen."

Rampardt sighed. He took a step toward his cruiser but stopped. "What I wish is he'd of listened to me before."

"To what? What'd you tell him?"

Rampardt turned and shone his light into the cab of the truck. Connor covered his eyes. "I told him what you never did," Rampardt said. "He's the one paying for it now. All the shameful times you let him be part of."

"You go to hell," Boyle said. "You got no right—"

"I got every right."

The fight came into Boyle like a jolt of voltage, and he lunged at Rampardt in a swift hot motion that washed off the watery drudge of sobriety. Rampardt blocked the swing with a solid forearm, his flashlight falling, and Boyle came back with a loose fist that grazed Rampardt's chest buttons. Then Rampardt got hold of Boyle's other arm and held it pinned between his own arm and chest. Boyle, squirming, misjudged where the prowler ended and fell off in front of it, Rampardt finally letting him go. Boyle hit the fir-needled deck hard and then lay sprawled out on his back, the dim stars blinking at him through the tree boughs. He stayed there until his heart stopped beating in his ears, and he sat forward.

"You come at me again, I'm using this," Rampardt said, his thumb on the scabbard of his pepper spray. "This isn't goddamn WWF wrestling out here."

Boyle pulled himself up by Rampardt's bumper and got to his feet. "I'm just trying to get by," he said.

"Well okay," Rampardt said, and he leaned forward to pick up his hat from where it had fallen. "Okay then. Aren't we all."

Connor had gotten out of his seatbelt and was sprawled across the bench seat twisting and crying when Boyle opened the door. Boyle sat him up and hugged him. "I'm okay," Boyle said, rocking him until he calmed. "He didn't hurt me."

The Eclipse rolling onto its side strained the Hino's engine into nearly stalling. From inside the cab, Boyle worked the winch slowly until the center of gravity shifted creak by creak and the car began to fall by its own power. The tires hit the ground with a squeal of springs and crunch of metal. In the headlights, pine needles and road sand exploded from under the Eclipse, rolling out so thick and smoke-like that for a panicked moment Boyle, twenty yards away, thought something had ignited the gas tank. Then the tiny debris started pelting the windshield, and he watched until the strange wind died off.

He and Rampardt stepped out of their vehicles at the same time. Rampardt came around and leaned on the Hino's fender. "Well, that was a sight," he said.

The rest of the job was busywork, and for a while Boyle surrendered his mind to it. The winch cable reeled back and the chains replaced in the toolbox, he walked up to the driver's window of the Eclipse and aimed his flashlight inside. He looked back at Rampardt.

"I need to straighten the wheel and put it in neutral," he said.

"Go ahead." Rampardt went back around and got in the prowler, where Boyle saw him talking on the radio.

It was easier to work from a seated position, and Boyle climbed in through the Jaws of Life hole in the driver's door. His canvas gloves still on, Boyle wiped safety glass off the driver's seat and worked the wheel around to get the tires straight. It took most of his arm strength—something must've been bent, or maybe one of the tires had gone flat. Then he took the transmission out of gear.

The Mona Lisa bag had dropped into the passenger seat, the rum bottle not far from it on the floorboard. He picked up the bottle and let himself imagine the tingle, the feeling of your skullcap removed and replaced with a warm towel. You let yourself think that a little in the evening will be enough, and that the erasing will last, but the want of it always came back sooner and stronger the next time.

He put it down and found the picture of Connor in his wallet, the one taken in the hospital, that stopped him all those times he needed a drink. He propped his flashlight on the dashboard and stared at the picture for a few moments, until he felt the familiar burn in his stomach. He found a pen in the car, and on the back of the picture he wrote, "18 years old. Driving Drunk." He took the Mona Lisa bag from the floor and put the picture on top of a checkbook inside.

Then he got out his cigarettes, half of them crushed from the fight, and started to light one before he remembered the gas. He thought about that night more than thirty years ago sitting and drinking with Rampardt in the front of his car. They were two grown men now, and no one could have told either of them what lay ahead.

A car door slammed behind him, and he climbed out of the wreck and met Rampardt between vehicles. "We all right, then?" Boyle said.

Rampardt looked at the ground between them. "It's finished," he said, and he cleared his throat. "Just keep on doing what you're doing, Mike." His eyes, blinking, were softer now. "I don't know what else to say." Then he looked out at the river and patted his hands together twice against the cold.

Boyle turned back to the wreck. As he was deciding the best angle to come at it with the slide-tray, something stopped him, and he looked over at the Hino's cab just as Connor tipped back in his seat. He was listening to music with his eyes closed and his face slightly skyward. Not sleeping but looking that way, in his own safe province that was constant and clear.

Charity

Wiping an orange shop rag between his palms, Vic Hardy hustled out of the bays to the parking lot. Royce, his new mechanic, was just climbing out of a hatchback with a cracked windshield and Louisiana plates. He was tattooed and jacked with muscle, his arms sloping out, his sandy-red hair gelled on top like standing flames. But he talked in gentle southern as he introduced himself and never averted his eyes, even when Vic asked about his prison record. "Methamphetamines," he said. "I opened the front door on hell itself."

Royce had made the drive up from the sodden rubble of post-Katrina New Orleans. It was the caseworker, Devona, who had talked Vic into taking a chance on him. She'd found the classified ad online and called to say that Royce was as hard-working and personable, as promising a candidate as Vic could hope to find. Her urgency roused images of the news he'd been watching all week, evacuees baking on shade-less sidewalks, t-shirts waving like white flags from water-lapped roofs. Vic had just turned fifty and, looking back on a decade of selfish living, found himself compelled by the idea of charity. Otherwise, he never would have shelved a stack of solid applications for the faxed resume of a man he hadn't met.

In the shop Vic introduced his other mechanics with short accolades. Mike Lorenzo had worked on Jeff Gordon's pit crew. Last year Eddie Cobb patented a carburetor-adjusting tool he optioned to Snap-on. Felix Diaz was the youngest ASE Certified Master Mechanic in Oregon.

"Damn," Royce said, shaking hands. "Y'all sound like a certified dream team."

"Let me see them tats," Eddie said.

Royce smiled uneasily and pulled up his shirt. Axes, flowers, names, *Ice Man. Unchained.* He was like a piece of mail that had been everywhere. Eddie and Felix unsnapped their shirts and showed their own. Checkered flag. Cougar head. *Wrap Your Ass in Fiberglass*, curling around a Corvette. Caught up in their fellowship Vic raised his own sleeve to the shoulder. From a stint in the army he had a narrow, rippling flag. "Old Glory," he said, feeling sincere with his kids—he thought of them that way. "That's the one that counts."

Later that morning, Mike Lorenzo tapped the open door to Vic's office on his way in. Vic had been trying to finish a parts order for nearly an hour, memories of his own agonizing trek to Oregon breaking his concentration. Royce was staying with his sister and didn't need an apartment, but Vic had started a list of tool distributors, Sears and Safeway locations, things he'd need to know. He looked up at Mike. "How's he doing out there?"

"I got him changing out the water pump on that El Camino. Looks like he more or less knows his shit." Mike sat in the vinyl chair across the desk and picked at a callus on his palm. "He say why he was in the clink down there?"

"First thing out of his mouth."

Mike scooted further back in the chair. After nine years here, he was owed full disclosure, but Vic was feeling superstitious. It seemed like a delicate fate that had put Royce in his hands.

Vic leaned over his papers and spoke calmly. "Eddie came to me on parole, and look how he's working out. What do you say we give the guy a clean slate?"

Mike laughed through the nose. Avoiding Vic's look he reached for an oil additive point-of-sale display on the desk. Three gears aligned vertically: Mike cranked the steel handle, bringing the tan fluid to the top. He stood up and turned toward the door. "Long as tools don't go missing," he said.

That evening Vic stopped at a basement jazz club near the

university, his usual refuge from the lonely hour before dinner at home with CNN. At the smallest booth in back he drank a first and then, more slowly, a second pint of stout.

In Connecticut his marriage had ended cruelly. To Carolyn he'd said things that alarmed him now to remember, and she'd said them right back. When she started fooling around he sold their Pepsi stock—a wedding gift from his parents—and left town. She'd always been after him to move across the country to Oregon. He drove aimlessly from state to state until, drunk outside Lincoln, Nebraska, he decided that living her dream would be the best way to punish her. So here he was.

Last year he'd received a short, loveless letter from his daughter, Amanda. She had given birth to a baby girl of her own. There was no mention of the father, and the return address was an apartment number in a town some ways south of where Carolyn and her new husband were living in Hartford. The envelope held two photographs of his granddaughter in her mother's arms. The wallet-sized one touched him. He hadn't spoken to Amanda in three years, since a phone call that ended with a litany of teenage insults he couldn't listen to.

He framed the larger photograph and hung it in the living room over the TV. He sent a check for a thousand dollars in a congratulations card he signed, Love Dad.

Royce's son came up by Greyhound as soon as Royce was settled. A freckly, red-haired seven year old, Sam soon became a fixture in the shop lobby, where he did his reading and workbook assignments after school. In the early evenings, his homework done, Sam would ask customers politely—sir, ma'am—if he could turn on cartoons. Vic remembered the ones he'd watched with Amanda: Loony Tunes, Care Bears, shows where animals ran the world. Now they were all humans, hyper people with big eyes who flew around and blasted lasers through outer space.

Some days Sam hung out behind the counter and helped Vic

with the bank deposits. Folding money excited the boy, and Vic showed him how to check twenties with the iodine pen, how to find the states written across the Lincoln Memorial on old five-dollar bills.

One night in particular convinced Vic that Sam and his father were fitting in. They were all in the lobby after work watching the Englishtown quarter-mile races on ESPN. Vic sipped his cream stout, Mike his porter, Eddie and Felix their lagers. Leaned over his knees watching the races, Royce pulled from a bottle of near beer.

Eddie was trying to tell a story about friends who'd gotten into a bar fight. He could barely finish for laughing. He held his flattened hand near his face and punched it again and again. "Bam," he said. "Bam. Bam. And that Morgan. I mean, he won't go down. Bam." He laughed his high windy laugh. "Bam, bam. Blood pouring out his nose. Out his eyebrow. But he's so fucked up drunk—"

"Eddie, can the language," Vic said. "The kid."

Eddie wiped his eye and nodded. "Sorry little man," he said.

Punching numbers into the calculator, Sam bumped Vic with his knee. "It don't bother me," the boy said.

Vic bumped him back. "It ought to."

"What's worse for cussing, Boo?" Royce said. "Around here or Aunt Suzi's cable?"

"Cable," Sam said.

"No getting around it," Royce said, shaking his head with anguish. "These kids today seen every manner of vice and sin before kindergarten."

On television a Hemi Cuda paired up against a Cobra Jet Mustang. The start light fell from amber to green, and eight seconds later the Cuda crossed the line at one-hundred seventy miles per hour.

"Arrest that boy!" Royce hollered. He turned from the TV. "Y'all run the quarter mile up here?"

"On pump gas or giggle gas?" Felix said, and Eddie interrupted:

"I ran high twelves in my old Formula."

"The hell you say."

"Me and my uncle ran eleven-four at one eighteen in his El Camino," Felix said. "Cam, headers and glass packs. Stock otherwise."

"God and little fishes."

Even Mike told about his '68 Hemi Challenger running low tens, the car in which Mike's best friend had hit a bridge abutment and was killed. Vic watched them talk. Like family around a dinner table, he thought.

October

Mornings in the locker room Royce brought his sleepy, staring, reticent coworkers to life with stories from the haunted bayous. Pulling on coveralls he talked about his grandmother's superstitions—always leaving a house through the door you entered, never borrowing salt, staring at the point of a knife to cure hiccups. He had a wart on his finger he rubbed with a raw potato. "Where y'at?" he'd say in greeting, having taught them all the proper Cajun response: "Ah-rite."

Business at the shop was good. With a big-block Camaro fetching sixty-thousand dollars, they catered to a new breed of hot-rodders who didn't know vise grips from channel locks, but who had the bank rolls to medicate their mid-life trauma with horsepower. Royce sold them engine chrome and beefed-up exhaust, increased displacement or more carburetion, often doubling the original estimates. In the lobby they shelled it out happily, as though he'd just done them an enormous favor.

It was Royce's way of speaking, Vic thought, unhurried and ruminative, always padding his pitch with "yessir" and "y'all," always good-natured with his humor. But when he followed up with customers after the work was done, Royce became pious with whole-hearted wonder at the miracle of engines. "Think for a second on everything going on inside there," he'd say, hands open on either valve cover as if he'd just performed a healing.

One afternoon, Vic brought Sam out to the Snap-On tool truck, where at the top of the rubber-coated steps Sam froze with his father's look of fascination. For thirty years, Vic had been running up tabs with these vendors—Snap-on, Mac, Matco—and suddenly, seeing it all through Sam's wide eyes, Vic remembered those first times boarding a tool truck, when he would tremble to think of himself in charge of such expensive gadgets. From magnetic strips on the walls and ceilings hung chrome ratchets and air tools, neon-handled screwdriver sets, mirror finish wrenches. Sam inched up on a rail that held the full spectrum of metric sockets, the first smaller than a pinky nail and growing by single millimeters to one the size of a soda can.

Sam picked up an engine mechanic's most trusted tool, a 3/8s swivel-head ratchet.

"There's a boy with the right instincts," Vic said to the owner of the truck, Mark, who was new to the route. When Vic counted out five twenties Mark looked relieved, as if he'd expected some kind of excuse.

"How much do you charge for this one?" Sam said, holding up the ratchet. Mark smiled at Sam but didn't answer until he saw the look Vic was giving him.

"That particular one," Mark said, "I believe costs thirty dollars."

Very carefully Sam placed it back on the magnetic strip. Vic turned back to take his receipt from Mark, but out of the corner of his eye he saw Sam lean over and give the ratchet a kiss on its smooth handle.

NOVEMBER

Sam walked into the lobby one afternoon, his jacket spattered with mud, carrying a handful of sticks tied with a shoelace. Vic was explaining an overhaul, and when the customer had gone he came around the counter and took the seat next to Sam.

"That a voodoo doll?"

"It's fixing to be." He carefully bent back sticks from the center of the bundle to indicate arms.

"Not of me, I hope."

"No, sir. Billy Cornelius." Sam took off his jacket and pulled the sleeve of his shirt up to the elbow to show a long pink scratch. "We was under the monkey bars and he tripped me on purpose."

"Now why would he go and do something like that?"

Sam shrugged. "He said I talk like a shit-for-brains."

Vic sighed and looked out at the sky through the lobby windows. The clouds were runny with frayed edges where sunlight fell through. "This Cornelius kid," he said. "I bet he gets picked on a lot at home. One thing about bullies, they always have it worse than you do."

Sam shrugged again. Vic asked to hold the doll, which resembled a person only in the vaguest sense. But better to take it out on this thing than to fight, he figured. He handed it back. "Who taught you that?"

"My momma. She does nice ones." When Sam looked up from the doll his face pinched. Like water sloshed from a cup, the tears ran down to his lips.

Vic stood and went to pour a bit of the hot water they set out for tea into a Styrofoam cup. "Follow me," he said and led the boy back to his office. They sat together on the old sofa. Vic dipped the bottom half of the doll, where the feet and waist would be, into the water. He had a small refrigerator in the corner, and when he set the sticks in the freezer box on top Sam scowled wickedly, and he laughed.

Over roach coach grinders the next day Vic asked Royce about Sam's mother. They were alone in the parts room. "We was Adam and Eve in the garden until this old girlfriend tracked me down," he said. "I like to hung myself when Maggie found out."

Vic wasn't surprised. Happiness excited desires, and suddenly you were tempted by the next thing. With his eager Huck Finn expressions, Royce made cheating and meth sound inevitable.

"I was a silver-lipped operator of bullshit," Royce said. "Nothing ever got through this thick old skull." He opened his hands on his knees and looked at Vic. "Man, you got a cigarette?"

Vic handed him his pack and lighter. "Didn't know you smoked."

"On and off since the age of nine." Royce drew on the cigarette until the tip blinked yellow. "Maggie," he said, lifting his pale eyes, likely seeing her in his mind. "She was too good for me was the problem." He dragged again and held the smoke deep inside.

DECEMBER

Royce overhauled his first engine, a '70 Le Mans 350, a week before Christmas. Vic had been watching him through the lobby window—covertly, so that Royce wouldn't feel nervous or untrusted. Aside from the engine removal and installation points, which took two people, the guys respectfully left him alone. Vic was hanging up a work order on the pegs as Royce tightened the last carburetor bolt. Royce double-checked the firing order, the rotor position with the timing mark on top dead center, and then filled the radiator with antifreeze. When he was finished he stood in front of the grille, glancing from point to point. Vic walked over and patted him on the shoulder. "Go on, son. Fire it up."

Royce waved Sam over from the lobby.

"You did it, Dad?" the boy said.

"I think I just might of." Royce opened the driver's door. "Maybe you better go ahead and turn the key, Boo. I don't have the guts."

The engine caught on its third spin, and Vic listened with his eyes closed for misfiring. After a minute watching the gauges with Sam on his lap, Royce got out and walked around to the fender.

"Oil pressure good?" Vic said.

"Good and high."

"Bring her up," Vic said. Royce reached under the hood and opened the throttle, the wind of the fan pushing his hair back. The engine revved smoothly and he smiled as though lolling in a tropical breeze. Sam hugged him from behind. "That's *sweet*, Dad," he said, and then there was applause from Felix and Eddie.

In a few minutes Mike came out from the lobby with the cordless phone. He handed it to Royce. "A lady for you. She said your sister told her to call here."

"Jesus." Royce mashed his hand against the receiver. "Maggie?"

"She didn't say."

Sam jumped in place and called out "Ma!" until Royce told him to pipe down.

"You know, that's probably long distance," Vic said.

Royce took the receiver into the parts room and Sam stayed with Vic. The boy reached into his pocket and pulled out his six five-dollar bills, his pay for sweeping the bays in the evening. "I knew she'd call," he said, folding an unfolding his money. "I asked for it in my prayers."

"Good timing," Vic said and pointed out the window to where the white Snap-On van was pulling up. Sam stared outside and then looked back at the closed door of the parts room.

"Better get going," Vic said. "Or you'll have to wait until next Friday."

When Royce finally came back, Sam had just disappeared into the van.

Royce set the phone down on a bucket of GoJo and stared at it like a man in shock. Vic was torn, his head telling him to mind his own business. "So, what she'd say?"

Royce looked up and blinked. "That she misses us."

"You and Sam?"

"Sure enough."

"Sounds hopeful."

"I don't know." He picked up the paperwork for the Pontiac. After a few moments of squinting at it, he set the clipboard on a tool tray. "I can't even remember how many hours this job took me."

The next morning Vic called Royce's caseworker and asked about Maggie. He mentioned possibly bussing her up to Oregon for a visit.

"What do you know about methamphetamines?" Devona said. The gravity of her tone made Vic realize how little he knew. He'd seen on the news some west-end houses raided, and the bloodshot, emaciated addicts rounded up out of the shadows like vampires. "But she finished her rehab," he said. "And Royce is clean from day one up here."

"It doesn't make them good for each other."

The phone in the crook of his neck, Vic stared down at a legal pad where he'd written MAGGIE in block letters. "You think she could get him started again?"

"Or the other way around. Or nothing could happen, I don't know. I have babies outside my door with missing parents, and you want me to worry about this?"

"I can cover the cost of getting her out here," Vic told Royce. A week had passed since the first phone call from Maggie. "Be happy to."

"How long would she stay?"

"You two could talk about that. As long as you wanted."

Royce wiped his forehead with his sleeve. He walked away from Vic, over to the bay windows, where he stared at the wet street colored by traffic lights. "You know what she said last night?

She wants to be enough for me this time. Isn't that something else? Her enough for me."

"Sounds like she's really thinking it through."

"It's like rapture and hell at the same time." Royce came back smiling but shaking his head. "I prayed to God she'd come back when I'd be able to take care of her." His eyes glassy, he looked at one of the words inked into his forearm. "I'd like to put some sandpaper to this goddamn skin of mine," he said.

JANUARY

On a drizzling northwest afternoon, Vic and Sam watched *Charlie and the Chocolate Factory* in Vic's office, Sam lying with his knees curled up on the sofa, his head on a throw pillow. The scene brought Vic back to a rented house in Hartford, his daughter beside him on a sofa, her plastic diaper crackling as she took raisins one at a time off his thigh.

"Any news at home?" Vic said.

"Well Ma keeps calling, so that's good. I guess they get to fighting a little, which isn't. You know."

"Fighting?"

Sam looked at him. "Not *fighting* fighting. Like he says, 'Who's this crawdad cook you keep talking about? Well, I can't help if I am.' Meaning if he's jealous a little." He looked back at the TV. "He just gets nervous sometimes."

In the movie a fat kid slurped dark chocolate from a lake. Then, reflected in the bottom of the screen, Vic saw a tiny Mike standing in a miniature doorway. Vic could guess what he wanted, but he didn't turn. He patted the boy's foot. "What's the word on Billy Cornelius?"

Sam shrugged. "He got mono. Has to take second grade again."

"You're kidding."

"The freezer's what done it," Sam said, never shifting his eyes from the television. It was as though what he had said were the most reasonable thing in the world.

"You mind if I steal Vic a minute?" Mike said, and Sam looked at him with eagerness and foreboding and said, "No, sir."

In the parts room, Mike handed Vic a printout of the month's recheck ratio. Thirty-eight percent of Royce's cars were coming back, far more than the other mechanics. "I just had one in with a loose head bolt," Mike said.

Vic stared at the sheet. "I'll talk to him. He's got a lot on his mind."

"Take a look at his fingernails all chewed up," Mike said. "His nose is always running. Maybe the guy needs to piss in a cup."

Vic pushed a hand through his hair. "You know, you can ruin him with that kind of talk."

"Vic, are you blind? I got two other guys to think about. He can't handle his recreational stuff, or he can't keep it recreational, then he's fucking up your reputation. He's fucking with *my* reputation."

The next morning Vic listened in as Royce talked to a customer, shamelessly embellishing the work he'd done. When the customer was gone, Vic walked up to him. "You're not going to get a tip out of that guy."

Royce began folding up the fender mat. "Tell me about it."

"He counsels vets for a living. He's on a tight income."

Royce lit a Winston—he'd been splitting cartons with Felix—and with the filter in his lips picked up a new spark plug. "He think his job's more important than ours?"

"Than fixing cars?"

"What we do here is no different than taking out cancer. Massaging hearts. Saving brains." He turned the spark plug but couldn't get the threads to catch in the cylinder head. He tried angle after angle. "I mess up, and there's a car that cuts out on the highway. Steering locks up, he kills not only himself but the van full of church kids in the next lane over. Nearabout anybody could tip something. I mean, even waiters. Who you ever heard of had his life saved by a waiter?"

Royce gave up on the spark plug. Leaning against an oscilloscope, he looked at a greasy thumbnail the way you might look at a French fry. Vic saw the black under the nail and thought, Don't put that thing in your mouth.

Vic was finishing the previous day's bank deposit, a job that should've been done yesterday. But he'd spent last evening in his office trying to draft a letter to his daughter. It began with, "Honey, now that you're starting a family of your own..." and went through seven rambling pages of apologies and warnings. When he'd finished he worried that she might find some or all of it offensive and shredded the letter, hoping to approach it with a clear head later in the day.

He had just gotten off the phone with a bank manager, who had noticed the missed deposit, when Royce burst into his office, his hand wrapped in bloody gauze. "How bad?" Vic said, knocking the calculator off the desk as he stood up. The roll of white paper trailed across the floor.

Royce's face was flushed and gaunt, like a man who had just finished a long, strenuous run. "It's pretty hairy," he said. "Header bolt snapped off. I think it about cut off a couple knuckles."

When Vic came around the desk, Royce stepped back and mashed the hand to his stomach.

It looked wrong. Vic glanced at the stain on the bandages. He was pretty sure it was transmission fluid. "You want to go to the hospital?"

Royce looked at the carpet. "I was thinking. This retired doctor fabbercated my sister a knee brace one time. He'd probably take a hundred bucks to patch me up. I go to the hospital, they jack up your liability."

"Let me see."

"Man, I told you," Royce said, all but yelling before he caught himself. "Now I just cut the living shit out of it. You can't ever get blood out of a carpet." Royce drew the hand in again, and Vic felt a great pity that precluded any chance of playing along.

When Royce glanced up Vic couldn't help but shake his head. "What are you doing, son?"

"Who says I'm doing anything?" Royce said, but it was empty, reflexive, and after a moment his face relaxed and he laughed disgustedly. "Man," he said.

"Come on, hey. It's forgotten."

Royce unwrapped the gauze and dropped it in the trash can.

Vic took in a breath "You talked to Maggie lately?"

"It's like interviewing for the toughest job in the world, every time." He watched Vic. "I can't calm down after."

"Yeah," Vic said.

Royce closed his eyes and laced his fingers behind his head. "I don't want to fuck up anymore."

The moment was a frail one, and as Vic struggled for meaningful words, he felt it lost. He bent over and picked up the calculator. When he straightened up, Royce was rushing out the door. Vic called his name softly, not wanting to alarm the customers in the lobby, and collapsed into his chair. He stared at the desktop for nearly a minute before he realized the deposit bag was gone.

When Vic called Sam's aunt she sounded tired and impatient and not very surprised. "He's done living here, then," she said. Vic put Sam on the phone and made out enough of their exchange to understand that Sam would be sent back to relatives in New Orleans.

After work Vic drove the boy to his aunt's house. The ride was a long one over the Willamette into Springfield, and Sam stared out at the sluggish traffic. The reflected rain, shadowed by freeway lights, moved across his face in oval coins.

"Mike shouldn't have let you hear all that," Vic said. "He was just talking. I wouldn't call the police."

"Don't, okay?"

"I promise."

"Because he'll have to go to jail all over again."

Vic said nothing and felt ashamed. He switched on the radio. All week NPR had been running special reports on Mardi Gras. He thought it might help Sam feel easier, but all he could find tonight was bluegrass music. He switched it off.

"Up here is nice," Sam said. In the buttery glow of the dashboard lights it seemed impossible, but he was smiling. "I'm glad we got to come."

"Well, you fit right in," Vic said, telling himself not to offer more promises—that he would find Royce and get him clean, that Sam might come back to stay for the summer. He allowed himself to feel satisfied.

They filled the rest of the ride with talk about things they had come to have in common—daytime programs, the likely engine size of the Pontiac in front of them, voodoo—until Sam pointed out the narrow street where his aunt's double-wide sat in a double-wide community. There were squat, square-cut azaleas and rhododendrons in front, porch lights burning, all of them trying hard to look like homes.

ABOUT THE AUTHOR

WAYNE HARRISON was an auto mechanic for six years in Waterbury, Connecticut, after which he worked as a corrections officer in Rutland, Vermont. His fiction has been featured on NPR's *All Things Considered*, and his short stories appear in *Best American Short Stories 2010*, *The Atlantic*, *Narrative Magazine*, *McSweeney's*, *Ploughshares*, *The Sun*, *Salon.com*, *Crazyhorse*, *FiveChapters*, *New Letters*, and other magazines. One story was Notable in *Best American Short Stories 2009* and another received special mention in *The Pushcart Prize 2012*. His fiction has earned a Maytag fellowship from the Iowa Writers' Workshop, an Oregon Literary fellowship, and a Fishtrap Writing Fellowship. His debut novel, *The Spark and the Drive*, was published by St. Martin's Press in 2014. He teaches writing at Oregon State University.